'Like t...

'Driving ...

'If you loved ...
Ham. It's that go...

'The unfortunate title chai...
the mind of Jim Bob. He's the
deluded wanna-be Princess Di fanat...,
Talent would refuse to audition'   *Leftlion*

'A book about the most annoying person in the world'
                    GEORGE BASS, *Drowned in Sound*

'Insufferably puerile'   *Time Out*

'There are also some brilliant illustrations that alone would justify
a "laugh out loud" quote on the back (although there are more than
enough laughs even without them)'   JOHN BRASSEY

'*Driving Jarvis Ham* is a darkly comic novel, hilarious in parts'
                    Independent on Sunday

'Rude, crude but hysterically funny'   *New Books Magazine*

'An idiosyncratic modern comedy for our times'
                    ANDREW COLLINS

By the same author

Storage Stories

JIM BOB

Driving Jarvis Ham

THE
FRIDAY
PROJECT

The Friday Project
An imprint of HarperCollins*Publishers*
77–85 Fulham Palace Road
Hammersmith, London W6 8JB

www.thefridayproject.co.uk
www.harpercollins.co.uk

This edition published by The Friday Project 2012

1

First published in hardback by The Friday Project in 2012

A catalogue record for this book is
available from the British Library

ISBN 9780007484652

Typeset in Minion by G&M Designs Limited,
Raunds, Northamptonshire
Printed and bound in Great Britain
by Clays Ltd, St Ives plc

MIX
Paper from
responsible sources
FSC **FSC™ C007454**
www.fsc.org

Jim Bob is an author, musician, father and occasional (once) musical theatre star. He lives in South London and holidays in Devon.

To Neil, for all the driving

If you're reading this it probably means I'm not dead.

'Would you drink a pint of your own piss?'

'Yes I would.'

'Eat some shit?'

'No problem.'

'How about someone else's piss or shit?'

'Yes.'

'Would you toss a man off?'

'Of course I would.'

'An old man?'

'Yes.'

'That old man who used to sit outside our school drinking white spirit?'

'Yes.'

'While your grandmother was watching?'

'Yep.'

'Would you punch a child?'

'Uh huh.'

A car game.

To pass the hours between service station stops and hard shoulder/weak bladder toilet breaks. To lessen the boredom that is the drive up from Devon to London with Jarvis Ham as a passenger.

The Million Pound Game is a hypothetical question game, like what would you do if you won the lottery or if you had three minutes to live or you were invisible.

Jarvis would always win the Million Pound Game. He would have tossed off a tramp while his nan watched. For a million pounds Jarvis would eat shit and drink piss. He'd punch a child. He'd kick the kid and stamp on its fingers while it was on the floor. Let's get this straight. Jarvis Ham would do it for less than a million. He'd do it for no money at all. Jarvis would do it for the fame.

Jarvis once told me that he had two big ambitions. Number one was that he wanted his life to become so unbearable, with all the fans and the stalkers and the photographers camped outside his house all night that he'd have to fake his own death. His other big ambition was to get shot dead by an obsessive Jarvis Ham fan.

True story.

Of course, if Jarvis did hit that kid I'd get two hundred grand. Twenty per cent of the million that Jarvis won for eating his own faeces or letting his grandmother watch him milk a tramp would be mine. I'd be a twenty per cent accessory to whatever filth or depravity Jarvis Ham put himself through to become a famous millionaire. As Jarvis Ham's manager: the punched kid, the poo, the wee, the perverted sex with the homeless, everything that I'm going to tell you about. It's technically one-fifth my fault.

PART ONE

The Ham and Hams Teahouse is one of five shops in a short row of businesses at the top of Fore Street. Inside it looks like an episode of the *Antiques Roadshow*. None of the furniture matches. The chairs don't go with the tables; teacups sit uncomfortably on odd saucers. Knives, forks, spoons and sugar tongs all come from different cutlery sets. If it actually had been an episode of the *Antiques Roadshow*, the expert would have said, 'If only you had the full set, I think, for insurance purposes, you would have been looking at fifty to a hundred thousand pounds. Unfortunately, what you have here is worth fuck all.'

The Ham and Hams Teahouse didn't care. Variety was its spice of life. The leaflets on the counter next to the big old Kerching! style till boasted about it: *The Ham and Hams Teahouse is not Starbucks*, the leaflets proclaimed above a drawing of an impossible cake.

Next to the counter there's a floor to ceiling glass cabinet that is a shrine to sugar. A cake castle. Half a dozen glass shelves packed with Bakewell tarts and carrot cakes, with sticky date, cream and treacle cakes. Big and high cakes topped with thick cream and fresh strawberries, looking like something the Queen might wear on the top of her head for the State Opening of Parliament. There are pineapple upside down cakes, victoria sponge up the right way cakes and tiramisu to die for. In fact, nut allergy sufferers have been known to play anaphylaxis roulette with a slice of chocolate and hazelnut panforte from the Ham and Hams Teahouse. From up to half a mile away, if you stood very still and quiet, you could hear customers licking their lips and saying 'yum yum'.

The flag of the day in the postage stamp of lawn in front of the Ham and Hams this morning was the flag of the Cook Islands: a blue background with a Union Jack in the top left hand corner and a circle of white stars to the right. There was hardly any wind and the flag was barely moving. A middle-aged couple dressed in shorts and matching sweatshirts sat beneath a pub umbrella at one of the two tables outside the Ham and Hams, they were eating the fluffiest scrambled eggs you've ever seen, served on the toastiest toast of all time. I parked the car and walked towards the teahouse.

I could see Jarvis through the window. He was wearing an apron with a picture of a big fat cartoon plum on it – no comment. He saw me and held up two fingers, he mouthed the words, 'two minutes' and carried on serving tea and cakes to the tourists. I stood in the street and waited.

A newly blue-rinsed old lady came out of the hairdressers next door to the Ham and Hams. She smiled and said 'hello' in that Devon friendly way that freaks out visitors from London who think it's some kind of a trick or a hidden camera show stunt. I smiled back.

'Lovely day for it,' the blue-rinsed lady said.

It was.

There were no paparazzi outside the Ham and Hams Teahouse this morning. No photographers on stepladders trying to get pictures of Jarvis through the window. Nobody jockeyed and jostled for position shouting 'Jarvis! Jarvis! Over here!' There'd be no warning of flash photography on the lunchtime news. Not today. The epileptics had nothing to worry about just yet.

The bell above the door of the Ham and Hams Teahouse tinkled and Jarvis walked out and straight past me like I was invisible. He was still wearing his apron. He headed towards my car. I sighed and aimed the key fob over his head, there was a beep beep and a flash of headlights.

'Don't cab me Jarvis,' I called out after him, and then more to myself, 'I'm not your chauffeur.' But he was already halfway into the back seat and closing the door. By the time I reached the car he'd already be snoring. He could fall asleep almost instantly like that, like he had a standby switch.

While Jarvis slept in the back I'd obey the signs and drive him carefully through the village, and as I left the village another sign would thank me for having done so. I'd drive carefully as requested through all the other villages and small towns on the way to the A38 – although I'd ignore the sign as I entered one village that someone had altered with white paint or Tipp-Ex to read PLEASE D I E CAREFULLY. I drove on through Yealmpton and Yealmbridge, Ermington and Modbury, seeing signs along the way for Brixton and Kingston: strangely West Indian sounding names for such very white places.

Turning onto the A38, I'd put my foot down. I could now drive less carefully. Make a mobile phone call, take both hands off the wheel. Open a bag of crisps, read a newspaper, start a 500-piece jigsaw puzzle of the Houses of Parliament.

I'd search for a radio station that wasn't playing sincere British indie guitar music, but I wouldn't find one and after going round the FM waveband in circles a few times I'd settle on some local news and an overlong, inaccurate weather forecast. I'd presume the weather forecaster was broadcasting from a windowless basement after travelling to work blindfolded in the back of a van. I could have told him it was actually an average day for the time of year. For any time of year really; some bright sunshine, with occasional

Simpsons clouds breaking up the otherwise pant blue sky. When we reached the outskirts of Exeter, just before we drove onto the M5 for the few miles of motorway that would take us to the A30 and the A303, it would rain. The radio weatherman was right there at least.

I'd look in the rear-view mirror at the sleeping Jarvis Ham. His chubby face flattened against the car window, his lips and nose distorted like a boxer captured in slow motion after a massive right hook. I'd try to work out what it was that made me not Jarvis's chauffeur. I just couldn't put my driving gloved finger on it. He always sat in the back. On all the many times I'd given him lifts I'd never once heard him call shotgun.

Giving Jarvis this latest lift from the South Hams up to London was going to be a more uncomfortable journey than usual for me, and maybe for him too. Not because the car was rubbish or because the roads were particularly bumpy. Far from it. The gearbox and the tyres were brand-new and the roads beneath them were smooth. The reason for my and perhaps Jarvis's discomfort was that we both had a secret we'd been keeping from one another. Jarvis's secret was that he'd been writing a diary. My secret was that I'd been reading it.

Mirror

Saturday 1 April 1972

BOY KING COMES TO LONDON

football this
and as many
first place in
a surprise to
big fans. Ian
without large

provocation.
howler and
discussion
ck in 1966.

GOAL!
not be the
r taking it
the worst
but not
and so
never"
alfway

The iconic burial mask of Tutankhamun was among the most
popular pieces in the Treasures of Tutankhamun exhibition.

Photo credit: David Davenglie

More than 1.6 million visitors are expec
to have visited the The Treasures of Tut
exhibition at the British Museum.

QUEUES
People queued for up to eight hours for
most popular exhibition in the Museum

ROYAL WORLD TOUR
At the end of September the exhibition
move on to other countries, including t
Japan, France, Canada and West Germa

**FOUR PAGE PULL OUT
WITH PUCTURES INSIDE**

NOT THE ONLY MUMMY IN TOWN

A Devon woman visiting the exhibition at the British
Museum went into labour yesterday (Friday) and gave
birth to a son in the museum's office. Disappointingly
the happy parents chose not to name their new
son after the Egyptian king and have instead
settled on the name Jarvis.

MARCH 31st 1972

Where were you born? Not the town or the country. The actual place of your birth, the venue? A hospital I bet. Or at home. Like Diana. She was born in Park House, Sandringham late in the afternoon on the first of July in 1961. She weighed a wonderful 7lb 12oz. I was born in a museum. And not just any old museum either. No way Jose. I was born in the British Museum. The British Museum. *I was born in the British Museum*! Imagine that. Mental. How brilliant was my birth. Correct. Very brilliant. And also, I almost forgot. It was Good Friday. How good a Friday is that? Correct again. Very good. More like Brilliant Friday. Very brilliant Friday. I don't know how much I weighed and don't say that you bet it was a lot or else.

Okay, so it's not exactly Samuel Pepys (although Jarvis will eventually bury a cheese during a fire).

It's not even a diary really. Not in the conventional sense. This first entry for example, can I call it an entry, even though I've just said it's not a diary, otherwise we'll be here all day? This first entry was written in black felt tip pen on the first page of a big purple

9

scrapbook. The newspaper cutting about the Tutankhamun exhibition and more importantly about Jarvis Ham's birth was glued to the front cover. On the next page of the scrapbook was the second diary entry. It's another Tutankhamun one. It's still not Samuel Pepys. Six years have passed. There's a title.

JARVIS HAM – BOY ACTOR

JUNE 20th 1978

My first ever acting role was the lead in our primary school's production of *Tutankhamun the Boy King*. I can't remember the story. Obviously. I was only six. I do remember that the rest of the class were all dressed as my slaves and they carried me into the dinner hall on a huge golden throne. I had to wave at the audience below me as they all cheered and applauded. My wave was like the wave the Queen Mother does. The Mayor and his wife were there in the audience and probably somebody from the local council. I was six, I can't remember all the details! All the mums and dads were there too and the teachers and headmaster and a vicar (a guess). I loved it when everybody was clapping and cheering. How do I remember that then, you're asking I bet. I don't know, but I do. I won a prize for my acting. Not an Oscar (not yet). I looked exactly like the real Boy King Tutankhamun did, even though I was six and he was nine. I hadn't trained at RADA or anything. I was only six. Have I made that clear? But, even though I was only six I definitely remember that it was brilliant. Very brilliant.

King Tut.

I got him that gig.

We were six years – although you probably already know that – old when our teacher Miss – can't remember her name – asked the class who would like to play the lead role. As she scanned the classroom for a raised hand I panicked. I thought she might not find a volunteer and pick me at random for the role.

'Jarvis, Miss!' I shouted out, pointing at Jarvis sat at the desk next to mine. The whole class turned to look at him as Miss thing thought for a moment, perhaps about how the cute kids always got to play the princes and princesses and maybe it was time to give the less fortunate uglier fatter balloon-faced kids a chance.

Why did the classroom seating have to be arranged alphabetically on our first day at school? Why couldn't we have been seated boy/girl/boy/girl instead? Then I might have been sat next to sweet freckle-faced Suzie Barnado. Who knows, perhaps we'd be married now. With a houseful of sweet freckle-faced kids. Or why couldn't I have just had a different surname? A name with its initial letter earlier or later in the alphabet. My stupid parents and their idiotic ancestors. If my surname had begun with an N or a P, I might have been sat next to Martin O'Brien on my first day at school. Martin O'Brien won three hundred grand on the lottery a few months ago. It was on the front page of the local paper. If my name had begun with an N or a P, I might have ended up managing Martin O'Brien instead of Jarvis and Martin would have had to give me £60,000 of his lottery cash.

The point is. I wouldn't have been sat next to Jarvis Ham when the teacher was looking for her boy king and we could all end this story right here and get on with our lives.

'Jarvis? Would you like to play the part of the Boy King?' Miss I-can't-remember-what-her-name-was said. She might as well have stood outside the school gates at home time and given Jarvis a free sample of heroin or crack cocaine.

Tutankhamun the Boy King would be Jarvis Ham's gateway drug.

Here's my review of the show:

There was an American actor and comic named Victor Buono. He played the comic villain King Tut in the 1960s television show *Batman*. Look him up on the Internet. I hardly remember Jarvis's King Tut performance, as I was only six myself, but for the sake of this anecdote I'm going to pretend that I remember the six-year-old Jarvis Ham's King Tut being a lot more like that thirty-year-old plump and slightly camp actor's version of King Tut than the ancient Egyptian boy child royalty that Jarvis was attempting to portray. I do remember that Jarvis had a beard that his mother had made from the inside tube of a toilet roll; it was covered in black and gold sticky paper and glued to his chin. His mother had also made the rest of his costume. She'd cut the top off a gold cocktail dress and made a headdress out of a tea towel that was held in place with a hair band wrapped in silver foil on top of her son's royal balloon head.

The rest of the class, including me, carried Jarvis into the dinner hall on a golden throne: made from the headmaster's office chair, covered in gold paper and decorated with hieroglyphics. It weighed a fucking ton.

It was not very brilliant.

After the performance was over our teacher congratulated us all for doing so well and she gave Jarvis a bag of Jelly Tots for his starring role. As we waited for our parents to pick us up and take us home Jarvis told me to hold my hand out and he poured six of the sugar covered jelly sweets into it.

My management commission.

Mister Twenty Per Cent.

* * *

The rest of the scrapbook was blank. What a waste of a good scrap-book. I suppose Jarvis might have started out with good scrapbook keeping intentions and then maybe he ran out of glue, or he lost his scissors. Or was this the beginning and end of the diary of Jarvis Ham? Just these two brief entries about the ancient Egyptian monarchy? Why couldn't I have been sat next to sweet freckle-faced Suzie Barnado? I could have been reading her diary. I bet Suzie had some filthy secrets.

Then I found this shoebox:

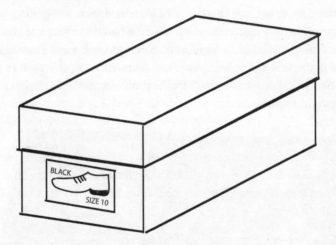

I climbed into the car, adjusted the rear-view mirror and looked at Jarvis fast asleep in the back; his face squashed against the window and the start of a dribble slowly chasing a raindrop down the glass. Not really, it wasn't raining, I'm just trying to insert a bit of poetry into the story. God knows it's going to need it. He had the seatbelt pulled across his body but not fastened. He said it made him feel sick when it was fastened.

There was a new smell in the car. I think you'd call it funky, funkier than James Brown. I turned my head to look. Jarvis had taken his shoes off. They were on the back seat next to his big fat plum apron.

These shoes:

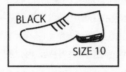

I thought about the shoebox and what I'd found inside it. There were some other newspaper cuttings. There were notepads and loose pieces of paper, stuff written on the backs of flyers and takeaway menus. I found a couple of photographs and some drawings, cinema tickets and hairdressing appointment cards and even one or two actual proper diaries. The shoebox was inside this huge old brown leather suitcase:

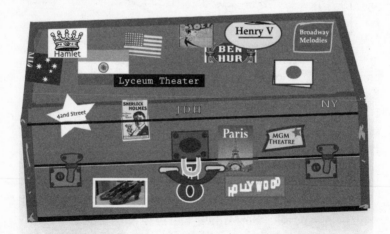

The suitcase had once been owned by an incredibly famous stage actor that I'd never heard of. Jarvis's father had bought it at an auction for his son's eighteenth birthday. It was covered in stickers of places in the world the actor had visited and the plays and musicals he'd appeared in while he was there.

In the suitcase with the shoebox there were two videocassettes, an Oscar statue, more notepads and books and various other bits of crap. It's this collection of junk that I'm calling Jarvis Ham's diary. It's more of a boot sale than a diary. A boot sale that Jarvis had been secretly keeping and I'd been secretly reading.

I imagine some people would think I was nosy. You should never read other people's private stuff. Especially diaries. Apart from anything else, you might find out things about people you'd rather not know about them. No shit Sherlock. *Now* you tell me.

As Jarvis's manager though, it didn't seem unreasonable to me that I should be entitled to read my client's memoirs. And it's memoirs that I imagine Jarvis would have liked to think that his collection of crap amounted to. Not a diary. Diaries were for teenage girls. *The Memoirs of Jarvis Ham* would be a seminal work of non-fiction that would one day be compiled, put into chronological order, published by Penguin or Faber and Faber and serialised in the Sunday papers. It would be read by a million Jarvis Ham fans and made into a Hollywood movie starring Tom Cruise with Jarvis himself modestly taking a cameo role as his own father. The Jarvis Ham memoirs would be a big fat doorstep of a book with black and white photographs. All it needed was some idiot to make sense of it all and put it into chronological order.

I opened a window to let the funk out of the car and I pulled slowly away from the Ham and Hams Teahouse and drove up Fore Street. We passed the ladies hairdressers: called simply, *Mary*, where both Jarvis and I had had our very first professional haircuts on a Saturday morning; when Mary would cut the hair of the young sons and grandsons of her more regular female customers.

We used to think there was something space age about the big hydraulic chairs at *Mary*, the way they moved up and down and the noise they made when they did so. The big hairdryers seemed pretty sci-fi too. Sitting in those big hydraulic space chairs we watched the old women in the mirror, reading their magazines with their heads drying inside what we imagined might have been space helmets or perhaps some kind of brain sucking gizmos, and for a while we believed that Mary and her customers were from another planet – which of course they were.

Next door to *Mary* there were two estate agents: a disproportionate amount for such a small village. When the tourists were full of tea and jam and clotted cream from the Ham and Hams Teahouse they'd waddle up Fore Street to look in the estate agents' windows. They were the only people in the village who could afford to buy anything advertised there.

At the top of Fore Street was the shop that sold everything else, from baked beans to condoms and everything in between. In the summer months the pavement outside the shop would be taken up with flip-flops and inflatable dinghies, and then during the tourist drought of winter they'd put out the Christmas trees and dancing Santas. Next to the shop there was a red telephone kiosk and a small post box on a stick. It was the one hundred and twenty-third building in the street, hence its piss your pants clever name: 123 Fore Street.

As I drove up Fore Street I stuck my head out of the window and breathed in the aromas of fresh baked bread and scones coming from the Ham and Hams Teahouse. I inhaled the powerful chemicals of the curly perms and demi-waves wafting out from under the astronaut helmets at *Mary* and the Hugo Boss on the cheeks and chins of the apple-faced young men who worked in the estate agents. If it were winter there would have been the scent of pine from the Christmas trees outside 123 Fore Street. But it was the end of summer and as I drove past I could smell the inflatable alligators and dinghies cooking in the August sun. I loved the smell of Fore Street in the morning. It smelled like victory.

I drove over a bump in the road and Jarvis's head bounced off the window.

'Are we there yet?' he said. He wasn't joking. It was one of his favourite car journey games: to repeatedly ask me whether we were there yet until I eventually lost my temper. Oh how we'd both laugh. This time though, Jarvis thought we might actually already be there yet. We'd been driving for less than five minutes.

'Not quite,' I said.

'If there's a shop,' he said mid yawn, 'I need to get some things.' And then he flicked his standby switch and he was fast asleep again.

Turning right at the top of Fore Street we drove past a church. There was a sign outside the church that read, 'Come Inside, the Holy Water's Lovely'. Hilarious. That was one of mine. If we'd driven in the other direction we would have passed a different church. The sign outside that church would have been 'They don't call Him God for nothing'. That was mine too. It's a stupid job but someone's got to do it. I also write jokes for 'luxury' Christmas crackers and ice-lolly sticks and the fortunes in novelty fortune cookies – stuff like 'This fortune will self destruct in five seconds' and 'Go home, your house is being burgled'. And here I am critiquing Jarvis Ham's diary. Jesus. Anyway, here's the third entry. There's been another jump in time – he's fourteen now – oh, and I can't apologise enough, Jarvis Ham is a terrible artist.

JULY 2nd 1986

DIANA

You came to Devon today
You opened a leisure centre
You pressed a button and turned on the flumes
You played snooker for the press
And then you went walkabout
You walked about past Milletts, past Marks and Spencers
People gave you flowers
And they sang happy birthday
I waited behind the barrier

I waited
I reached out
You touched my hand outside the Wimpy Bar
And then you were gone

His poetry is diabolical too.

I was in Exeter with Jarvis that day. No drawings from me though. Or poems. I could write one now I suppose.

DIANA

You came to Devon today
You opened a leisure centre
You pressed a button and turned on the flumes
You played snooker for the press
And then you went walkabout
You walked about past Milletts, past Marks and Spencers
People gave you flowers
And they sang happy birthday
Jarvis waited behind the barrier
He waited
He reached out
You touched his hand outside the Wimpy Bar
Where I was eating a Spicy Beanburger
With chips
And then you were gone

I don't feel good about it now. I know I missed out on a big local occasion and being a part of history, especially with what would happen in Paris and all that, but I wasn't really a big Diana fan and certainly not a super-fan like Jarvis was. Jarvis loved Diana, worshipped her, and after she touched his hand in Exeter when he was fourteen he thought she probably loved him too.

I had just become a vegetarian at the time though, and Wimpy had recently launched their Spicy Beanburger – they were the first UK burger chain to sell a veggie burger. Teenage vegetarians living in small Devon villages in the nineteen eighties didn't get a lot of opportunities to eat veggie burgers. So while Jarvis waited patiently for his princess to come, I ate like a king. A burger king.

It was a busy day in Devon for Diana. She opened the leisure centre and a supermarket and a library. She turned on the water in the swimming pool, setting the flumes and wave machine in motion. She played snooker: being applauded by all the patronising local big cheeses and yes-men for holding the cue the wrong way and making a foul shot. Then after that Diana had lunch at the Guildhall, watched a pageant depicting one hundred and fifty years of the police service, before finally going on a walkabout, culminating in her touching local dignitary Jarvis Ham outside the Wimpy.

When Diana opened the leisure centre she unveiled a plaque, the plaque would later on mysteriously disappear. It was a big local news story. People were outraged. The plaque was never found.

Yes that's right, you guessed it. I found it in the shoebox.

Not really. I didn't. God knows where the plaque went. It has nothing to do with this story.

By the way, when Jarvis wrote about his birth and glued the newspaper cutting about Tutankhamun into the scrapbook I imagine it wasn't done at the actual time. The language he uses is pretty childish – it's a writing style that Jarvis will stick with for most of his life – his writing may come across at times like it's being dictated by a child who's just learning to read out loud in front of the rest of the class. Expect quite a lot of *And there was a man. And his name was Roy. And Roy had a dog. And it was called Rover. And Roy had a stick. And Roy threw the stick. And Rover fetched the stick.* That kind of thing. Sorry. Don't shoot the messenger.

Anyhow, the way Jarvis has written about his birth may be childish but the cutting out and the gluing is beyond the abilities of a nought year old. The same goes for the bit about his first acting job.

The Diana poem, however, happened live. Jarvis wrote it when he was fourteen. And the drawing. He showed me them both at the time. I remember lying about how good they were.

It was the same day that Jarvis had come out to Ugly Park with me to talk to my evil stepfather Kenneth about him perhaps getting a job or doing the washing up once in a while, or better still, getting out of town so me and my mother could return to the single parent/ only child domestic bliss that we'd been perfectly happy with before he'd shown up.

Ugly Park – okay, *Ugbury* Park – was a small council housing estate on the outskirts of Mini Addledford, the village where Jarvis and his parents lived. It was like a theme park – its themes being urban decay and inner city depravation. At weekends and on Bank Holidays people from the surrounding villages would drive out to Ugly Park to ooh and aah at the dogfights and the graffiti and to film the boy racers on their camcorders as they bombed around the estate in their stolen cars before crashing them into a wall and torching them.

That's not true. I'm exaggerating. But for the six months that my mother's boyfriend Kenneth moved in that's what it felt like. It felt like this:

And what I really wanted it to feel like was this:

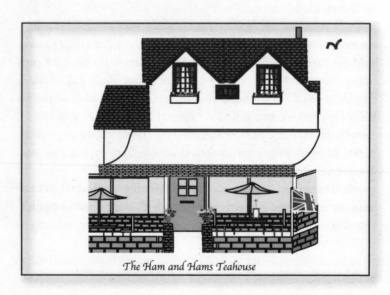

The Ham and Hams Teahouse

I would have loved to have had a mother who made costumes for me and a father who baked cakes and wasn't drunk in an armchair all day long, burning holes into the upholstery while he fell asleep watching the horse racing with a fag on.

And then there was the bullying.

I've compiled a typical week's worth of Kenneth bullying episodes into one fun-packed omnibus edition to illustrate.

It was a Tuesday. I came home from school, mum was at work and Kenneth was in the front room, drunk, sitting in his armchair – that used to be my armchair – and shouting abuse at Basil Brush. I went into the kitchen and made an elaborate sandwich from the ingredients I'd bought on the way home from school (there was never any food in the cupboards at Ugly Park). I took my sandwich into the front room and as I made my way past Kenneth towards the sofa he leant over and took the sandwich off my plate and stuffed it into his mouth. When I complained Kenneth raised his hand, showing me the back of it in a way that was supposed to tell me he'd hit me with it if I didn't shut up. He'd never catch me I thought. It would probably take him half an hour to get himself out of the armchair. But I couldn't be sure. And even if the backhanded slap didn't hurt, the nicotine stains on Kenneth's fingers would probably give me cancer.

I sat down on the sofa and opened my bag of crisps and can of Coke. Kenneth leant over again and snatched the crisps from me and crushed them into a bag of Cheese and Onion crumbs before handing them back. He then launched himself out of the armchair with the aid of a massive fart and walked off to the toilet to piss all over the toilet seat and floor, putting his cigarette out in my can of Coke along the way.

Kenneth would never bully me in front of my mother and when I tried telling her about it she thought I was making it all up because

I was missing my real father. I wasn't. He was no Atticus Finch or Doctor Huxtable either.

You know how when you're young there are people you call your aunt or your uncle even though they aren't related to you? Jarvis's parents were like a mum and dad version of that. Which would have made Jarvis my brother I suppose. Okay, bad analogy. But while Kenneth was living with us at Ugly Park I spent more time with the Hams than I did at home. I liked the pots of tea, the biscuits and the cakes. I liked the family board games, the Charades and the I Spy. There was an open fire in the living room and food in the kitchen cupboards. Jarvis's house always smelled of freshly baked bread and flowers. Ugly Park smelled of ugly.

Sometimes I'd go to the Ham and Hams with Jarvis after school and I'd feel so at home that I'd forget to go home.

One day I went back to Ugly Park after sleeping the night in the spare room at Jarvis's house and there was a fire engine outside my house. Kenneth had set fire to the kitchen. The fire brigade had found him asleep in the armchair, fifteen feet of ash hanging from a cigarette on his bottom lip and children's TV on.

He had to go.

So Jarvis and me bunked off school one afternoon and went to Ugly Park to talk to Kenneth. I was too scared to confront him on my own and taking Jarvis with me seemed like a good idea (the only idea) at the time.

I knew my mother would be out at work and Kenneth would be drunk and half asleep on the sofa when Jarvis and I walked into the front room. When Kenneth woke up and saw us both standing above him, all menacing and purposeful, he'd be terrified. I imagined this is what Kenneth would see:

In reality, it was more like this:

Kenneth woke and he stood up – faster than I'd ever seen him move before – and perhaps it caught Jarvis unawares, because I doubt he really meant to slash Kenneth across the arm with the cake slice that he pulled out from inside his jacket. There was a bit of black-currant jam on the cake slice; it was made of stainless steel, a bit like this:

I don't know why Jarvis had come tooled up. Or cutlery-d up, and I don't know what he was expecting to do with the cake slice. It didn't even have a pointed end. What was he going to do? Ice Kenneth?

Which shows what I know about cutlery.

The cake slice cut into Kenneth's arm like it was a blancmange and Kenneth's blood sprayed onto both Jarvis and me.

We were blood brothers now.

We ran away from Ugly Park, all the way back to the Ham and Hams – throwing the bloody cake slice into the river on the way, like we were in a gangster movie. We washed the blood off in the bathroom at Jarvis's house and Jarvis's dad cooked us dinner. We didn't talk about what had happened with Kenneth, although we were both expecting the police to knock on the door at any moment. They never came.

After dinner we played Monopoly with Jarvis's mum and dad and I let Jarvis buy Mayfair and Park Lane because they were his favourites. I stayed the night in the spare room but didn't sleep.

When I went home the next day my mother was alone. Kenneth had left Ugly Park – via Accident and Emergency – saying to my mother that her son and his friends were all mental.

Ugly Park didn't seem quite so ugly any more.

None of that was in the scrapbook or the shoebox.

In fact, other than Jarvis's birth, his first acting job and meeting Princess Diana outside the Wimpy there was no record of any other event in the shoebox or the suitcase for the first eighteen years of Jarvis's life.

I could fill in some of the gaps for him of course. There are a lot of gaps. I could tell you Jarvis was picked on a bit at school. That might be important, I don't know. He was called Piggy and Pork Ham and Fathead, and that was just by the teachers. I'm joking of course. The other kids did take the Mickey out of Jarvis but it didn't seem to bother him all that much.

What else? Jarvis was neither an underachiever or an overa-chiever at school. Academically at least, he was average. He wet himself in the classroom twice that I'm aware of, but that had more to do with bad teachers on a power trip putting the fear of God into schoolchildren if they ever dared ask to be excused for five minutes to go to the toilet.

He loved drama at school. From the day that Miss whatever-her-name had chosen him to play Tutankhamun he wanted more. He didn't get picked for any further lead roles though and he had to be content with being a king carrier like the rest of us, but he loved it anyway. Jarvis liked dressing up in the ludicrous costumes his mother made and talking in even more ludicrous accents and voices.

At secondary school there were fewer opportunities for his acting skills. There was no proper drama department and Jarvis always said his English teacher didn't like him and so never picked him for any of the end of term productions.

In his last year of school he took a lot of days off with made up illnesses and on the final day of the last term he went home early before all the tears, shirt signing and flour and egg fights. He said that people had been throwing eggs and flour at him at school for the last five years so why would he choose to stay around for another afternoon of it voluntarily?

Jarvis had no brothers or sisters but he did have two parents – one of each – and when he left school he started working full time with them in the Ham and Hams Teahouse.

At weekends Jarvis used to put on little shows for his parents in their front room. He had a magic set, with a top hat and a wand and a collapsible card table that he'd cover with black cloth to put all his tricks on. He was a shit magician if that helps the story.

Jarvis also did impressions of people from TV and had a terrifying looking ventriloquist's dummy called Ronnie that his dad eventually had to get rid of as it gave Jarvis's mother nightmares. There's an old photograph of Jarvis with Ronnie on the mantelpiece in the Hams' living room, and if I was cruel – which I'm afraid I am – I'd say that when I looked at the photograph, I found it difficult to tell which one was the ventriloquist and which one was the dummy.

On Jarvis's sixteenth birthday his mother was rushed to hospital with breathing difficulties. After two weeks in hospital she was in a wheelchair for a while. I hilariously used to refer to her as A Mum Called Ironside. Jarvis always laughed, so that was okay.

Perhaps by being reticent with the diary action for the first eighteen years of his life Jarvis has actually done us all a favour. Nobody really likes that opening twenty or thirty tedious pages of a too big celebrity autobiography when the author bangs on about their childhood and about what their grandparents did in the war, when all we really want to read about is the up to date juicy stuff with all the famous people and the sex and the drugs and the fighting.

If the gaps in Jarvis's adult life really do annoy you though, why not fill them in yourself. People are mad for audience interaction these days. It might even be fun. In those months in 1992 for example, when not much happened because Jarvis was busy reading this book:

Why not imagine he was playing football for England instead.

Or on the unfilled diary pages of 1993 and 2002 you could pretend he was building an ark because God had told him in a dream that a big flood was going to wash Devon into the sea, or you could pretend he was baking a massive cake for the Queen or something. Seriously, go ahead. Make it up. I wish I had.

But perhaps you honestly can't be bothered to do that and you'd just prefer the truth, no matter how dull.

In the first half of 1993 Jarvis was flying model helicopters and blowing up balloons at a toyshop and for nearly all of 2001 to 2010 he was depressed. There. It's this year's *Bridget Jones*. Call Hollywood.

Right. Let's get on with the sex, the drugs and the fighting.

I turned up the in-car radio to drown out the in-car snoring, adjusting the volume knob like I was cracking a safe. Turning it up loud enough to drown out Jarvis's snoring but not loud enough to wake him up.

If a fast song came on I'd put my foot down and accelerate with it. I knew these narrow B roads like the back of my hand. I knew the high hedges and the telegraph poles. The farmhouses, the churches and derelict barns converted into open plan holiday homes. I knew the village post offices and which farm shops sold fresh eggs and cheese, and which sold honey and strawberries. I knew where the trees on either side of the road would appear to bend over to touch each other's fingertips, creating a tunnel over the road. I knew when we were coming up to a red telephone box or wooden bus shelter. Cows. Horses. Sheep. Potholes and pigsties. That's what the back of my hand looks like.

I'd driven down this particular road hundreds of times. I could take the curves and corners at speed, like a rally driver. I knew where the really narrow parts of the road widened slightly in case I needed to pull in to let an approaching vehicle pass. I could drive with my eyes closed. I could take my hands off the wheel and let my mind do the steering. Sleep-drive: navigating by driving over the cat's eyes and potholes. My car could read Braille; it's these new tyres. At the moment I was stuck behind a tractor.

* * *

I waited for the road to widen so I could overtake. I watched blades of straw rain softly down from the back of the tractor's trailer onto my windscreen. I heard Jarvis, sensing the car's drop in speed, shifting restlessly in his sleep in the back seat. I was really hoping to get as far into the journey as possible without him waking up. In many ways I was like a new and exhausted parent transporting an insomniac newborn baby. *Don't wake up, don't wake up.*

I looked at the petrol gauge. The needle was practically on the E. Why hadn't I filled up before I left? I tapped the gauge with my fingertip but it didn't move. I rocked side to side in my seat hoping that might shift the petrol about in the tank and give me a few more miles. The needle stayed on the E. I was going to have to stop for fuel. Arse candle. If I stopped at a garage Jarvis would definitely wake up. Balls.

The tractor turned off and I overtook. The tractor's driver waved as I passed. I waved back. I didn't know him. This is Devon.

The nearest petrol station was next to a closed down Mister Breakfast. The rusty sign was still there outside the boarded up roadside restaurant. With its picture of a cartoon chef in a wifebeater string vest, a knife in one hand and a fork stabbed through a sausage in the other, welcoming passing hungry drivers in with his toothy grin. Mister Breakfast had a big droopy moustache and a chef's hat. He looked a bit like the Swedish chef from the *Muppet Show*. Someone had spray painted the word 'cock' on his hat.

As I pulled into the petrol station next door to the closed down restaurant, I felt – what does nostalgia feel like? – I don't think it was nostalgia.

JANUARY 16th 1991

Today was my first day working at Mister Breakfast. I had to show customers to their tables, take their orders and bring them their meals. I've done this all before of course at the H and HTH (the Ham and Hams Teahouse, abbreviation fans). It's what people call a busman's holiday (I think). I also had to make the toast and I burned it three times. Geoff the chef (that is honestly Geoff's name) said that famous people sometimes come in to eat here. Mostly rock bands. And sometimes people from the television or a whole rugby team. Imagine if Diana came in. I wouldn't know what to do. It would be brilliant though. I wouldn't burn her toast that's for sure.

I worked at Mister Breakfast with Jarvis back then. It was my first ever job. The uniforms looked ridiculous. That's what I remember most. Stupid hats. I think we were supposed to look American. We didn't. We had to wear a badge that said Master Breakfast – including the female members of staff – until we were mature and qualified enough to fry stuff without setting fire to Devon, and then and only then would we be allowed to call ourselves Mister Breakfasts and get a new badge. Christ, such aspirations and dreams, I'm surprised our young heads didn't explode at the thought of it.

JANUARY 30th 1991

Geoff says because of my experience working in a teashop since I was twelve I can cook breakfasts now. It's only frying eggs and sausages and bacon and using a microwave but standing behind the counter in the kitchen where all the customers can see you, I suppose it's a bit like being an actor

on a stage and the customers are the audience. Being a chef
is like being a film star.

Yes Jarvis, a film star. That's exactly what it's like.

Tom Cruise in *Cocktail*. That's what he was thinking of.

Jarvis liked to spin and flip the ketchup and brown sauce bottles
when Geoff wasn't looking, throwing them into the air and catching them behind his back, on the off chance Princess Diana might
drop in for a Full American English or a plate of pancakes and a pot
of tea and think she was being served by Tom Cruise. Jarvis had
made me take a bus into Plymouth to watch *Cocktail* with him
three times when it came out. I hated it slightly more each time.

During my time at Mister Breakfast I never got to cook anything
but I did have to handle an abattoir worth of dead animals in spite
of my vegetarianism and I swept the floors and cleaned the toilets.
The pay was pitiful. The soft toy Mister Breakfasts I had to embar-
rassingly try to flog to the customers looked like they'd been won
at the worst fair in the world and were probably held together with
pins and asbestos and stuffed with bandages and nappies. The
souvenir t-shirts with their slogan 'I Got My Fill at Mister Breakfast'
would prove to be in particularly poor taste after what was to
happen there. Maybe that would have made a better slogan: 'Mister
Breakfast – In Poor Taste'. They could have had it printed across the
front of their stupid hats.

Nobody had heard of the Breakfast Killer back then, those shirts
and soft toys are probably going for a fortune on Internet auction
sites now. If only I'd saved a few. Oh well, hindsight is a wonderful
thing.

I worked at Mister Breakfast for nearly a year and in all that time
neither Princess Diana nor anyone off the TV or a single recognis-
able rugby player ever came in to eat any of our disgusting food.

* * *

I stopped the car at one of the small petrol station's pumps and switched off the engine.

'Are we there yet?'

FEBRUARY 12th 1991
JARVIS HAM MY TOP TEN
FAVOURITE THINGS

1. Diana
2. Drama Club
3. 'Ice Ice Baby' by Vanilla Ice
4. Tom Cruise
5. Gummy Bear Sweets
6. The Simpsons
7. Singing
8. My Aviator sunglasses
9. Prince Charles
10. Neighbours (the television programme)

I filled the car up with petrol and went into the shop to pay. Jarvis was already there, standing by the crisps jigging from one foot to the other.

'The toilet's broken,' he said.

I looked at the man behind the counter. He had his back to us as he filled a shelf with cigarettes.

'Flooded,' the man said without turning to face us. Even without seeing his face it was obvious the man was in a foul mood about something.

Jarvis tilted his head and looked at me like a puppy that had just eaten my homework, and even though Jarvis was in his late thirties and not my developmentally challenged son, I asked the man behind the counter, 'Can't he just pop in quickly?'

'Not unless he's got flippers and a snorkel he can't,' the man said before finally turning round to face us. 'What pump number was it?'

The friendly Devon ways that freaked out visitors from London must have bypassed this petrol station. I looked through the window at the minuscule garage forecourt and its two petrol pumps. Mine was the only car there.

'That one,' I said, pointing at it.

'Number one,' the man said. 'Forty pounds and a penny.'

Jarvis was now doing the quick march on the spot and also grabbing the front of his trousers. I gave the man behind the counter two twenty pound notes and he made a show of holding them both up to the light and examining them.

'There's a lot of forgeries about,' he said and looked at me, 'And a penny.'

I rooted around in my pockets for a bit and then gave him another twenty pound note.

'Can I have a receipt please?' I said.

Jarvis left the shop in a hurry as the man behind the counter slowly counted out my change in as many small denominational coins as possible.

I walked back to the car where Jarvis was still hopping from foot to foot.

'Go in the trees,' I said.

'Someone might see me.'

I looked around. Apart from the fast passing cars and Devon's grumpiest man in the garage shop there was nobody about.

'Will you keep a look out?' Jarvis said.

I followed him over to the trees behind the closed down Mister Breakfast and stood with my back to him as Jarvis relieved himself.

'Remember when we worked here?' I said.

'No.'

'Yes you do.'

'When?'

'You used to spin the sauce bottles.'

'The what bottles?'

'The sauce bottles.'

'I did?'

'Yeah, like Tom Cruise.'

'Tom Cruise?'

'In *Cocktail*.'

'Don't remember.'

'You do.'

Jarvis came out from the trees, still zipping his flies and looking down at the front of his trousers.

'For a million pounds …' he said.

'No. I wouldn't.'

Why couldn't I have been sat next to sweet freckle-faced Suzie Barnado?

JARVIS GOES TO DRAMA CLUB

MARCH 8th 1991

Drama Club was brilliant tonight. We played a game called Meeeooowwwmmm Screeech! where we stood in a circle and passed a toy car around. If we had the car and somebody shouted Screeech! we had to quickly stop and pass the car back in the opposite direction. We also played another game where we stood in a circle and one person had to leave the room and while they were gone one of the others would be made leader. When the person came back the leader would do small movements and the others would copy him and the person who'd left would have to guess who the leader was. It's difficult to explain on paper.

MARCH 15th 1991

At Drama Club tonight we sat in a circle, Pamela started a story and threw a tennis ball to one of us. When we caught the tennis ball we had to carry on the story. I would have been brilliant at this but I'm rubbish at catching.

MARCH 23rd 1991

At Drama Club last night we made a short list of ideas for our spring production for Local Heroes of History Month. It's going to be brilliant. Very brilliant.

MARCH 30th 1991

Tonight everybody stood in a circle and one of us had to be a murderer and one of us a detective. The murderer had to kill everyone else by winking at them and the detective had to guess who the murderer was before they'd killed all of Drama Club. Just before it was time to leave Pamela told everyone to stand in a circle for a new game. She told us to close our eyes. The next thing that happened was everyone started singing happy birthday and when I opened my eyes Sandra had brought in a birthday cake for me. I blew out the candles and everybody cheered and someone started shouting 'Bumps! Bumps!' but I don't like the bumps and so they let me off. It's not actually my birthday until tomorrow but I didn't let that spoil it.

APRIL 6th 1991

I was very disappointed to not get the role of Sir Francis Drake in Drama Club's production of *El Draco* for Local Heroes of History Month.

The actual medium of delivery of that last entry probably tells us more than the words themselves. I've taken it out of context. Here it is back in the context I found it.

```
                          Jarvis Ham
             Ham and Hams Teahouse
                         Fore Street
                    Mini Addledford
                              Devon
```

```
Pamela Finch Masters
The South Hams Am-Dram Players
The Hall
Parsonage Road
Devon
```

6th April 1991

Dear Pamela,
I was very disappointed to not get the role
of Sir Francis Drake in Drama Club's
production of *El Draco* for Local Heroes of
History Month.

Yours faithfully
Jarvis Ham

PS: I feel I can no longer attend Drama Club

After Jarvis leaves Drama Club the diary action goes quiet for a bit.
And then this is published.

JUNE 7th 1992

And then it all goes quiet again, because Jarvis has always been a slow reader.

Until.

DECEMBER 2nd 1992

DIANA (REVISED)

When you came to Devon that day
To open a leisure centre
When you pressed a button and turned on the flumes
When you played snooker for the press
And then when you went walkabout
When you walked about past Milletts, past Marks and Spencer
When people gave you flowers
And they sang happy birthday
When I waited behind the barrier
When I waited
When I reached out
And most of all when you touched my hand outside the
Wimpy Bar
And then you were gone
Were you sad then?

We've just turned onto the A38, onto the Devon Expressway. The trees are now too far apart to touch each other. If you look out of your window to the left you'll see Dartmoor in the distance. There's a jack-knifed artic and traffic backed up behind it over on the right, London and the North are up ahead and Jarvis Ham is in the seat behind. He's reading *The Stage* newspaper. He's taken his shoes off again.

These shoes:

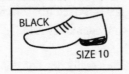

The Devon Expressway. It sounds a bit sci-fi doesn't it, like it's a monorail across the moon or something.

It isn't.

The A38 is a major English trunk road that runs for 292 miles from Bodmin in Cornwall to Mansfield in Nottinghamshire and the Devon Expressway is a forty-two-mile stretch of the A38 between Plymouth and Exeter. It's not important.

'Actors wanted,' Jarvis says, reading out loud from *The Stage* (the newspaper, he's not *on* a stage – God forbid). 'To be represented by an exciting new agency and personal management company.'

'You know those things are always a con. They just want your money.'

'Okay,' Jarvis said and scanned the ads again. 'Lookalikes wanted then. Who do I look like?'

'*Whom*,' I said.

'Okay. *Whom* do I look like?'

I looked at Jarvis in my rear-view mirror: my Jarvis-view mirror.

'How about Elvis?' he said.

I looked at his balloon head and his baby face. His rainbow coloured hair and bright red hospital radio DJ glasses.

'Maybe if he was still alive.'

'What?'

'Who knows what direction he would have gone in,' I said, 'if he'd lived. The fourth age of Elvis.'

'What?' Jarvis said.

'After Young, Movie and Vegas Elvis.'

I looked at his face in the mirror again. 'Objects in the rear-view mirror may appear closer than they are' it said on a transfer at the bottom of the mirror. Jarvis looked up from his newspaper.

'Do you think he's really dead?' he said.

'Huh?'

'Elvis. Do you think he's really dead or that he faked his death?'

'No. He's dead, definitely dead. The King is dead,' I said. 'Or on the moon.'

'That didn't happen.'

'Pardon?'

'The moon landing,' Jarvis said.

'*Landings.*'

'What?'

'*Landings.* There've been six manned moon landings.'

'Really? Six?'

'Yep.'

'They didn't happen,' Jarvis said in a way that told me there could be no argument about it. 'For a million pounds,' he said. 'Would you fake your own death?'

'I sometimes think I already have.'

'What does that mean?'

'I don't know Jarvis. I just said it. Thought it would sound clever. Surely you have to be famous to properly fake your own death anyway.'

'If you were famous then, for a million pounds would you fake your own death?'

'If I was famous I probably wouldn't need the money.'

Jarvis hated it when I didn't take his games seriously. I looked at his balloon head inflating in the rear-view mirror and to avoid it bursting and ruining my freshly valeted car seats with Jarvis brains, I decided to play along.

Sort of.

'There's no way Elvis faked his death,' I said. 'Apart from the fact that he surely would have picked a more heroic cause of death than sitting on a toilet eating a peanut butter sandwich if he had faked it, apart from that, if Elvis was still alive he would have said something by now just to put a stop to all the people impersonating him, especially the shit ones, which is nearly all of them. Did you know

– and I'm making some of the facts up because I can't remember them – but there are around one hundred thousand Elvis impersonators in the world. There were only a hundred and something at the time of Elvis's death. If this rate of Elvis growth carries on, by 2019 a third of the world's population will be Elvis impersonators.'

'Are you just saying this to sound clever as well?'

'No, it's true.'

'Well, anyway,' Jarvis said, but didn't finish what he was going to say and went back to reading the job ads in *The Stage*.

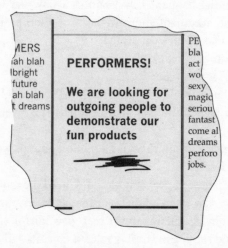

You know how some people desperately want to get into the music business and so they get a job in a record shop? Or how actors work in call centres selling boiler maintenance cover and serve cocktails on roller skates wearing a tight t-shirt with no bra because it's good acting experience? I mean: have you looked at the acting job ads in *The Stage* lately? Those are the only vacancies you'll find there. Croupiers wanted for cruise ships, strippers and pole dancers needed urgently. Six pages of vacancies for door-to-door mobile phone salespeople and high street charity muggers, and maybe one acting job, that's unpaid and has already gone.

In 1993 Jarvis got a job demonstrating – and mostly crashing – remote controlled helicopters into the floor of a toyshop and making unrecognisable balloon animals in the hope that it would be his big break into acting, one small step onto the yellow brick road that would eventually lead him to being presented with a real version of this piece of misspelled tacky plastic:

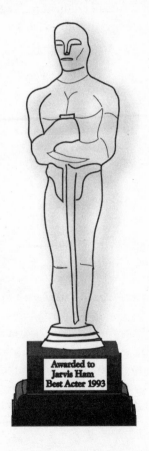

Awarded to
Jarvis Ham
Best Acter 1993

Jarvis had it made for himself at Southamleys toyshop when he was working there as Devon's worst toy *demonstrater* – it was in the old actor's suitcase. The job ad from *The Stage* was in the shoebox. There was also a *1986 Charles and Diana Fifth Royal Wedding Anniversary Diary* in the shoebox, where I found the next series of diary entries. At last, a bit of love interest.

Because the diary is for the wrong year all the days of the week are wrong.

JARVIS GETS A GIRLFRIEND

> **JENNIFER FER**
> **HOW CAN I HELP?**

MONDAY ~~SATURDAY~~ NOVEMBER 8th ~~1986~~ 1993

After a boring amount of time spent working in the most boring job in the whole boring world something happened that wasn't boring. There's a new girl who works in the food hall at the garden centre. And she looks like Diana. (Lunch = fish fingers, chips and peas)

THURSDAY ~~TUESDAY~~ NOVEMBER 11th ~~1986~~ 1993

I stood in the longer queue at the food hall yesterday because the girl who looks like Diana was working on that till. The queue was so slow I nearly didn't have time to eat my lunch. (Lasagne)

MONDAY ~~SATURDAY~~ NOVEMBER 15th ~~1986~~ 1993

Some schoolboys came into the shop today and stole the helicopter I was flying. They just snatched it out of the air and ran away with it. The manager called the police but they didn't catch them. The funny thing is they won't be able to fly the helicopter because I still had the remote control, ha ha ha.

WEDNESDAY ~~MONDAY~~ NOVEMBER 17th
~~1986~~ 1993

Chose the slow and long Diana lunch queue again. (Some pasta dish or other)

THURSDAY ~~TUESDAY~~ NOVEMBER 18th
~~1986~~ 1993

Today those schoolboys came back and stole the remote control.

FRIDAY ~~WEDNESDAY~~ NOVEMBER 19th
~~1986~~ 1993

I think the name badge of the girl who looks like Diana says Jennifer Fer. I didn't want to look too long in case she thought I was a sex pervert. (Fish cakes)

SATURDAY ~~THURSDAY~~ NOVEMBER 20th
~~1986~~ 1993

Jennifer Fer (that's definitely her name) (Shepherd's pie and a banana milkshake) (Not together)

SUNDAY ~~FRIDAY~~ NOVEMBER 21st ~~1986~~ 1993

Helping Dad in the teahouse today because Mum is ill. Kept thinking about Jennifer Fer.

MONDAY ~~SATURDAY~~ NOVEMBER 22nd ~~1986~~ 1993

No Jennifer Fer in the food hall today.

TUESDAY ~~SUNDAY~~ NOVEMBER 23rd ~~1986~~ 1993

Still no Jennifer Fer.

Uh oh, another poem.

TUESDAY ~~SUNDAY~~ NOVEMBER 23rd ~~1986~~ 1993

Jennifer
Jennifer
Jennifer Fer
Jennifer
Jennifer
Jennifer Fer

Obviously a work in progress.

WEDNESDAY ~~MONDAY~~ NOVEMBER 24th ~~1986~~ 1993

Jennifer is back! (Mushroom stroganoff)

THURSDAY ~~TUESDAY~~ NOVEMBER 25th
~~1986~~ 1993

Jennifer gave me an extra roast potato with my lunch today. She had tinsel in her hair. And extra gravy (Not in her hair) (On my plate) (ha ha). After work I went to watch a local DJ switching on the Christmas lights in the village. They'd built a small tower from scaffolding and he stood on a platform on top of the tower next to a lady from the council and together they pulled (or pushed) a switch and the lights came on. It was rubbish. I wish Jennifer Fer was there though. One day I will have to come back by aeroplane from Hollywood or somewhere to turn on the Christmas lights in my old village. Maybe Jennifer Fer will be with me. But maybe she'll be called Jennifer Ham then.

FRIDAY ~~WEDNESDAY~~ NOVEMBER 26th
~~1986~~ 1993

Jennifer sat at the same table as me on her coffee break. There were lots of other emptier tables she could have sat at instead. So it must have been her deliberate choice. She said hello and I said hello but then I had to say goodbye straight away as I was going to be late back at work. She smelled of Fruit Salad chews. (Can't remember what I ate)

SATURDAY ~~THURSDAY~~ NOVEMBER 27th
~~1986~~ 1993

At lunchtime someone set off the fire alarm in the food hall and we had to all go and stand outside until the fire brigade came. When we were outside Jennifer Fer came up to me and asked me what my name was and where I worked and things like that. I told her I demonstrated model helicopters at the toyshop next door, although I was really an actor and it was good practice for performing for the public. (Sausages, green beans and potatoes) ((Left to go cold on table during fire alarm)) (((It wasn't me who set off the alarm just so I could talk to Jennifer Fer))) ((((Although it would have been a brilliant idea if it had been))))

SUNDAY ~~FRIDAY~~ NOVEMBER 28th ~~1986~~ 1993

Helping Dad again. Dropped a trifle and Dad started to cry a bit. I think it's because Mum is ill. Kept thinking about Jennifer.

TUESDAY ~~SUNDAY~~ NOVEMBER 30th ~~1986~~ 1993

ST ANDREW'S DAY
Jennifer came and watched me fly helicopters.

WEDNESDAY ~~MONDAY~~ DECEMBER 1st ~~1986~~ 1993

I was in the lunch queue and Jennifer Fer pinched and punched me for the first of the month. (Shepherd's pie)

THURSDAY ~~TUESDAY~~ DECEMBER 2nd ~~1986~~ 1993

I'm taking Jennifer out on Friday!! (Baked potato and coleslaw)

'Could we have a table by the window please?' Jarvis had asked the rather handsome young waiter when he came in through the restaurant doors with Jennifer Fer as though he was some Hollywood big shot and it was a packed out exclusive and impossible to get a table in sort of restaurant.

It wasn't.

'Your usual table? Certainly sir. Can I take madam's coat?' the rather handsome young waiter said. Jennifer took off her green waterproof raincoat and handed it to the waiter, who looked around for a cloakroom or a coat hook on which to hang it.

There wasn't one.

The not packed out not exclusive and not impossible to get a table in sort of restaurant had no cloakroom or coat hooks. It was a Mister Breakfast. The same Mister Breakfast Jarvis Ham had not long ago left to pursue his acting career (demonstrating remote control helicopters at a toyshop on the edge of a field between a farm shop and a garden centre on the A38 half a mile away). The same Mister Breakfast where I was still working. Still working, still not cooking. Still only Master Breakfast. Yup, you guessed it Poindexter. That rather handsome young waiter was me.

I showed them to a table by the window. Where the sun had faded the Formica tabletop and somebody had carved the word *DIE* into it. I would have pulled Jennifer Fer's chair out for her but it was bolted to the floor. I folded her raincoat over the back of the chair, gave her and Jarvis laminated menus – also faded in the sun – and took out my order pad.

'Drinks?'

I brought them their drinks and their meals and I acted like the perfect waiter and kept up the pretence that Jarvis was a local big shot to help him impress his girlfriend. And how could she not be impressed by a man who chose to walk her, in the pouring rain, dodging the speeding traffic and exploding puddles, along the busy slip road from the garden centre to one of Britain's worst roadside restaurants for their first date?

As they were eating their dessert I refilled the tomato shaped plastic bottles and wiped the egg yolk and gravy off nearby tables so I could eavesdrop. They seemed to get on like a house on fire.

'I think I'll make acting my life,' Jarvis said as he poured Jennifer Fer a fresh cup of tea and the lid of the stainless steel pot flipped open and tea spilled onto the table and flowed slowly into the grooves of the word *DIE* – you didn't get this kind of stuff at the Ivy.

While Jennifer watched the tea Jarvis stared at her name badge like he was a sex pervert or something. She was still wearing her food hall uniform and still had tinsel in her hair. She'd been serving Christmas dinners all day in the garden centre's vast food hall to coach loads of old ladies on turkey and tinsel days out and she hadn't had time to change. She looked nothing like Princess Diana by the way.

'It wouldn't fit,' Jennifer said, catching Jarvis staring at her name badge. 'My actual name. It's Jennifer Ferminalitano. So they short-ened it. Plus, there was another Jennifer already working in the food hall. Although, you know, I think really they couldn't pronounce it or be bothered to learn how. Do you know where the ladies is?'

'Ferminalitano? Is she from somewhere exotic?' I asked Jarvis while Jennifer was in the ladies.

'Totnes.'

He's funny isn't he, Jarvis Ham. Look at him in the back of the car there now, reading his show business newspaper. Still daydreaming his daydreams. Look at him there, off in a world of his own. With his funny coloured hair and his hospital DJ glasses. Jarvis the loveable clown. Aw, isn't he sweet. Maybe you even feel a bit sorry for him.

Don't.

Seriously, don't.

You'll feel stupid later on.

Drivers rarely get carsick. It's something to do with focusing on the road ahead and so not seeing things contrary to what their inner ear perceives. Something like that. Thinking about this next 1993 diary entry almost made me the exception that proved that rule.

WEDNESDAY ~~MONDAY~~ DECEMBER 8th ~~1986~~ 1993

Went for a walk through the garden centre with Jennifer after lunch. We stopped under some mistletoe and kissed.

Bleeeuuurrgghh. Somebody open a window.

THURSDAY ~~TUESDAY~~ DECEMBER 9th ~~1986~~ 1993

Jennifer had drawn a heart shape with cream in my tomato soup today.

Seriously, someone open a window.

FRIDAY ~~WEDNESDAY~~ DECEMBER 10th ~~1986~~ 1993

John Major has said that Diana and Charles are separating. I think some of the stuff in that horrible book may have been true. Diana must have been so desperately unhappy. I feel sick if I think about it too much. I hope what's happened to them never happens to Jennifer and me. It will *never* happen to Jennifer and me.

SATURDAY ~~THURSDAY~~ DECEMBER 11th
~~1986~~ 1993

I tried to talk to Jennifer about Diana today but she said she wasn't really bothered. I told her about the book I'd read and about how Diana was unhappy all the time and how she cut herself with a lemon slicer and deliberately fell down stairs and I suggested that Jennifer might like to read the book but she said she didn't. She said she's a republican and the Royal Family are all a waste of money. I thought we were going to have our first argument. I hope John Major wasn't going to have to make an announcement about us (that's a joke).

WEDNESDAY ~~MONDAY~~ DECEMBER 15th
~~1986~~ 1993

PRINCE CHARLES BAPTISED IN THE MUSIC ROOM
AT BUCKINGHAM PALACE (1948)

I crashed a helicopter into a child's face today by accident. The child's father complained to the manager and I was moved to filling helium balloons 'for my own safety and everybody else's' until next week.

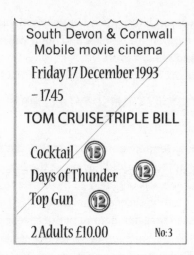

South Devon & Cornwall
Mobile movie cinema

Friday 17 December 1993

– 17.45

TOM CRUISE TRIPLE BILL

Cocktail ⑮

Days of Thunder ⑫

Top Gun ⑫

2 Adults £10.00   No: 3

TUESDAY ~~SUNDAY~~ DECEMBER 21st ~~1986~~ 1993

I'm back on the helicopters. The manager said (exact quote),
'In all my years in this bloody business nobody has ever
burst quite so many balloons as you did last week Jarvis.'
Jennifer said that I should be proud as (exact quote number
2), 'It's nice to be a winner.'

FRIDAY ~~WEDNESDAY~~ DECEMBER 24th
~~1986~~ 1993

It's been very busy at work. I can't wait for Christmas.

SATURDAY ~~THURSDAY~~ DECEMBER 25th
~~1986~~ 1993

CHRISTMAS DAY

I wish Christmas would end. Jennifer. I miss her so.

SUNDAY ~~FRIDAY~~ DECEMBER 26th ~~1986~~ 1993

BOXING DAY BANK HOLIDAY (UK & EIRE)

3am. I can't sleep. Jennifer wasn't in the food hall at lunchtime today. I should have asked one of the women working there where she was but I didn't. I think she doesn't work on bank holidays.

MONDAY ~~SATURDAY~~ DECEMBER 27th ~~1986~~ 1993

Jennifer wasn't there again. I asked a woman who was clearing tables. She said 'Jennifer? Is she a relative?' I said she was my girlfriend and the woman looked at me funny. She then went away into the kitchen and came back with the other Jennifer, who was about sixty years old. I explained everything and the sixty-year-old Jennifer said that Jennifer Fer has left because the turkey and tinsel offer is finished and she was only there for that. I panicked and left.

TUESDAY ~~SUNDAY~~ DECEMBER 28th ~~1986~~ 1993

At the food hall they wouldn't give me Jennifer's address or phone number because it's confidential. How can it be confidential? It's a food hall, it isn't MI5 or something. I crashed a model helicopter into the ground in the afternoon (on purpose).

WEDNESDAY ~~MONDAY~~ DECEMBER 29th
~~1986~~ 1993

> Why didn't she leave a note or tell me she was leaving? I
> don't understand. I asked more questions in the food hall at
> lunchtime. They told me they couldn't help me and gave me
> her name badge. I don't know why.

It was in the shoebox.

There were about seven thousand people living in Totnes in 1993. If we stood outside Woolworths for long enough we'd eventually find Jennifer Fer. At some point, everybody is going to need some pick 'n' mix. Instead, we walked up and down the steep hills and looked in cafés, in second-hand bookshops, chemists and charity shops. We went to the library and walked along the river and stood on the centre of the bridge and looked up and down stream for her. We hiked back up the steep hill to the castle and looked down over the rooftops below, hoping we might see Jennifer Fer in her back garden putting out the rubbish or feeding a Christmas robin.

We didn't find her.

'You're not going to like me for saying it,' I said to Jarvis. 'But there really are plenty more fish in the sea.'

'I hate the sea.' I was right. He didn't like me for saying it.

'Why didn't you get her address?'

'I don't know.'

'Or her phone number?'

'I don't know.'

'What now?'

'I don't know.'

And then Jarvis saw this in the window of a candle shop:

DARTMOOR OR LESS THEATRE GROUP

Are looking for boys and girls aged 8 years – 16 years
(Height restrictions may apply) for the Spring musical
production of

Oliver!

Those interested should come prepared to sing and
act and be available for performances to take place
in the final two weeks of March 1994

OPEN AUDITIONS

**Thursday 6th January 1994
6.30pm
Civic Hall, Market Square
TOTNES**

WEDNESDAY ~~MONDAY~~ JANUARY 5th ~~1987~~ 1994

1.30am. I. Can't. Sleep. Too. Excited. *Oliver* auditions tomorrow
(or rather today).

Hang on a minute. What about Jennifer Fer?

THURSDAY ~~TUESDAY~~ JANUARY 6th ~~1987~~ 1994

EPIPHANY

Ladies and gentlemen … Jarvis Ham will play the Artful Dodger in *Oliver!*

Well, all the local talent must have still been in panto because I honestly don't know how else Jarvis managed it. I went with him to the audition and when we joined the queue outside the Civic Hall we looked like we were in the wrong one. We were too tall and too old for a start. We had more in common with the pushy parents than their wannabe-by-proxy children.

During our long and complicated series of bus journeys to Totnes for the audition Jarvis entertained – in heavily inverted commas – the other passengers with his cockney accent and singing – in even heavier inverted commas – the songs from *Oliver!* that he'd spent the past few days frantically learning. His cockney was at best an unconvincing Australian and his singing was appalling.

When the producer of the musical interrupted Jarvis's audition annihilation of 'Consider Yourself' to tell him, 'We'd like to offer you the part of Dodger. How are you fixed for February and March?' I thought it must be a hidden camera show or a *Springtime for Hitler* style get-rich-quick-with-a-deliberate-theatrical-flop scam.

It wasn't.

The lunatics gave him the role.

It was the beginning of a new year and a new decade, the final week of Jarvis's Charles and Di-ary: 'Epiphany' the diary said. And even though I've used the word in one of my witty church signs: 'Get Some Karmic Relief (Epiphany Peculiar or Epiphany Ha Ha)', I still wasn't totally sure what an epiphany was. I looked it up.

epiphany |ih-pif-uh-nee|

noun (pl. -nies) (also Epiphany)

the manifestation of Christ to the Gentiles as represented by the Magi
(Matthew 2:1–12).

• the festival commemorating this on January 6.

• a manifestation of a divine or supernatural being.

• a moment of sudden revelation or insight.

I'm pretty sure Jarvis will have thought the last two bullet-pointed definitions applied directly to him. And two months later, the second he stepped onto the stage as the tallest, oldest and chubbiest ever Artful Dodger and said to Oliver Twist in his best Dick Van Dyke, 'Wotchoo lookinat?' the audience of parents and pensioners and tourists sheltering from the rain would have surely known they were witnessing the manifestation of a divine or supernatural being. It was Jarvis himself who was having the sudden revelation or insight. He believed he was about to follow in the footsteps of Phil Collins, Davy Jones, Steve Marriott, Elijah Wood, Ben Elton, Robbie Williams, Tony Robinson and all the others who'd begun their successful showbiz careers playing the Artful Dodger on stage.

FRIDAY ~~WEDNESDAY~~ JANUARY 7th ~~1987~~ 1994

Handed in my notice at Southamleys. I'm going to be a star!!

But really though, *what about Jennifer Fer?*

SATURDAY ~~THURSDAY~~ JANUARY 8th ~~1987~~ 1994

Began the day with muesli and a vocal warm up.

Ha ha, Jarvis was a jobbing actor now. There was no time for girl-friends. No sir. After the success of the *Oliver!* audition we rode buses up and down and along the side roads of the A38 to a series of open auditions and read-throughs he found advertised in newspapers, shop windows and on leaflets pulled from library notice boards. The Devon Expressway was Jarvis Ham's Broadway. The village halls and scout huts were his West End.

Here are a few of the posters and flyers Jarvis kept. They should really be spinning towards us like newspaper front pages in a movie montage, preferably accompanied by a muted trumpet riff.

ACTORS WANTED
For new production

SECRET IDENTITY
OF THE BARD

Casting Call
6th March 11am
DARTINGTON HALL

A BRAND NEW PRODUCTION
OF A BRAND NEW PLAY

Could this be the role for you?
Ring Gavin: 01753 99~~~~~~

Details Gavin? *Details?*

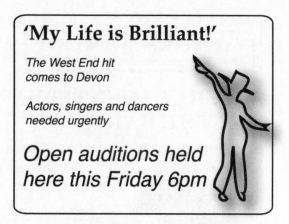

'My Life is Brilliant!'

*The West End hit
comes to Devon*

*Actors, singers and dancers
needed urgently*

*Open auditions held
here this Friday 6pm*

ACTORS!

Have you got
what it takes
to help us
solve the
case?

sleuth

To audition:
Contact the production company
Little John, Bertram & Barry
01767 000090

Jarvis forgot about Jennifer Fer and concentrated on his mono-
logues and audition songs; honing his craft. He had singing lessons,
learned how to breathe properly and paid over the odds for some

moody publicity photographs. He memorised passages from the classics: from Shakespeare and Chekhov, Tennessee Williams, Arthur Miller and also some of the scenes from his favourite movies. He practised in front of the mirror and in front of me: developing his range of looks and emotions. Jarvis Ham forgot about Jennifer Fer and worked on his accents, he learned all about motivation and how to write a good acting CV. Every day he carried out a routine of facial stretches and tongue twisters: *Mommala Poppala Mommala Poppala, a proper cup of coffee from a proper copper coffee pot.* If only someone had told him you can't polish a turd.

18 March 1994

OLIVER! South Devon Young Duchess Theatre
◆✧✧✧

The production was perhaps too ambitious for such a small space. The song and dance routines seemed under rehearsed and messy. The casting was bizarre. In particular, the young and yet obviously too old for the part actor playing the Artful Dodger was so miscast as to almost be in the wrong theatre. What were the producers thinking? The – and forgive me if this sounds cruel – rather unfortunate looking actor stood literally head and shoulders above the rest of the orphans and pickpockets on stage, the tall scruffy top hat balanced on his head merely adding to the absurdity of the situation. All this could be forgiven if he

```
could sing, which unfortunately he couldn't.
I'd do anything to not have to see this
production ever again.

Brian Fallstop
```

Surely even the most glass half full optimist would find it hard to see anything positive in that review. Ladies and gentlemen …

MARCH 18th 1994

I have just read the newspaper review for last night's show. It isn't as good as we would have hoped but journalists are not allowed to write anything nice. Also, it was the first night. Everyone was nervous. If he came back in a week the review would be a lot different. Even if he came back tonight, it would be different. Tonight's show will be brilliant. Very brilliant.

Oh dear.

MARCH 18th 1994

Arrived at the theatre this evening and was told the show was cancelled.

The Dartmoor or Less Theatre Group had managed what the producers of *Springtime for Hitler* had failed to do and closed their awful show on its opening night. Before Jarvis had had the chance to read Brian Fullstop – sorry, Fallstop's – stinker of a review they were already on their way to the airport with suitcases stuffed full of investors' cash.

You're probably thinking, forget about Brian, what about me? I'm really no better than Brian with my turd polishing remark. Brian was just doing his job. You're thinking I'm not much of a friend. I know that's what you're doing. You're starting to feel sorry for Jarvis again. I told you, don't. You will feel stupid later on.

Plus, my unkindness is retrospective. At the time I was ridiculously supportive. I was the one who stood in the rain waiting for the bus to take Jarvis to the next audition for another acting role he had no hope of getting. I hung around for hours in cold church halls and musty rooms above libraries with all the other nervous parents while he auditioned. I helped him learn his lines. I was the Fagin to his Artful Dodger and the Juliet to his Romeo. I was ridiculously supportive. I told him he was good when really he was bad. I bigged him up when he probably could have actually done with a bit of smalling down. If I'd pissed on Jarvis's chips in the early days we might not be in the mess we're in now. I should have Simon Cowelled his dream before it had time to recur.

Incidentally, you can't polish a turd – you can however cover it in glitter.

Jarvis asked me to meet him after his appointment at *Mary* – when the going gets tough, the tough go to the hairdressers – he said he had something important to tell me: something to do with his show business career. I went to the Ham and Hams Teahouse next door to the hairdressers and found a seat at a table near the window.

The flag of the day from Jarvis's dad's collection, flying almost imperceptibly in the small garden out front, was the white cross and red and blue rectangles of the Dominican Republic. It was one of his dad's favourite flags. There had been half an hour's worth of snowfall that morning and the grass outside the teahouse was covered in a carpet of white. It would have made a nice postcard. I ordered a cream tea from Jarvis's mum and waited for her son to finish his ride in the hydraulic space chair next door.

When Jarvis came in to the Ham and Hams his hair was layered and parted on the side. It was blonde. He sat down opposite me and brushed flakes of snow from the top of his head.

'Bloody kids,' he said.

I was staring at his new haircut. I may have been open mouthed.

'Do you like it?' Jarvis said, and turned his head so I could get the full 3D effect.

'You're blonde,' I said, just two words away from being speechless. I think Jarvis must have gone into *Mary*, said to Jean, 'Could you do it like this please.' And then presented her with this picture:

Mrs Ham came over with my cream tea. She put it on the table and looked at her son, assessing his new do, his Lady Dye. She sighed/nodded/smiled and nodded again. And then she kissed the top of his newly blonde head and walked away to serve a group of ramblers.

Jarvis watched his mother for a moment, then turned to me. 'I don't want to work here all my life.' He said.

'Okay,' I said. I was still distracted by his new hair and also the food on the table. The Ham and Hams served the best cream tea in the whole of Devon. The huge heart, diamond and star shaped scones, packed with fruit and served with freshly clotted cream and an assortment of homemade jams in little pots.

'I've been thinking that maybe the stage isn't the right medium for me,' Jarvis said.

I licked my lips. I wasn't really listening. My bottom lip tingled, as if remembering what the scones had tasted like the many times I'd eaten them before and preparing itself for that sensation again.

'I think it might be time for a change of direction,' Jarvis said.

'Right,' I said, slicing the heart shaped scone in two and covering each half with clotted cream.

'I want to concentrate more on my television career.'

'Sure,' I said, adding a spoonful of strawberry jam onto the cream and stuffing the scone into my mouth.

JUST THIS ONE LAST LIFT
AND THAT'LL BE IT

Me and my girlfriend argued last night. She said I'd spent way too much of my life worrying about Jarvis. 'Tell me about it,' I said. Which was a schoolboy error because she then told me about it for fifteen minutes. She said Jarvis had treated me like his unpaid chauffeur for years. 'I know,' I said.

'Why doesn't he drive himself?'

'He can't.'

'He won't more like.'

'He doesn't know how.'

'Why doesn't he learn?'

'I don't know.'

Silence.

'This is the last time,' I said.

'Did you save his life in the past or something?'

'Eh?'

'Like in the ancient Chinese proverb, when you save someone's life you become responsible for that person for ever.'

'I don't think that's an ancient Chinese proverb.'

'Whatever.'

'I know about Chinese proverbs.'

Nothing.

'I write them,' I was referring to the novelty fortune cookies.
More silence.
'I think it's actually from *Kung Fu*.'
Still nothing.
'The ancient Chinese children's TV series.'
Silence + moody stare.
And then my girlfriend said, 'He's weird.'
Checkmate.

I wanted to say that it was a guy thing and that men stick by their friends no matter how needy or annoying they are, in a way that she'd never begin to understand. I thought about mentioning Kenneth and the cake slice. How Jarvis and me – and technically Kenneth too – were blood brothers. But I didn't.

'Just this one last lift and that'll be it.'
'Really?' she said.
'Yes.'
'Promise?'
'Promise.'
'What if his life needs saving?'
'I wouldn't piss on him if he was drowning.'
'That doesn't even make sense.'

And I told her, yes, I know it doesn't, and then I kissed her and not that it's any business of yours and it has nothing to do with this story, but we had sex.

My earlier weather forecast was almost bang on. We were not far from the outskirts of Exeter, not far to go to the M5 for the five miles of motorway that would take us to the A30 and it had started to rain. Ignoring for a moment the dangers of skidding on the wet tarmac and aquaplaning into the central reservation, I really liked being on a major road in the rain. I liked it when it suddenly went dark in the middle of the day. It felt like the world was about to end and yet I was somehow safe inside my car, and there were all those television science shows I'd seen as a child that had taught me that I was in the safest place if lightning were to strike.

I liked the sound of the rain as it crashed into the car's metal and glass and I found the rhythm of the back and forth of the windscreen wipers comforting. Especially if a song came on the radio with almost the same tempo as the wipers and there'd be that moment when the beat of the song and the beat of the windscreen wipers would become one. Maybe I'd tap along with my fingers on the steering wheel and then I'd imagine the bass player in the passenger seat joining in with a finger slide down the strings and then the guitarist in the back seat would join in too and we'd be rocking in time with the back and forth of the windscreen wiper beat. Then the wiper tempo would slip out of time with the song on the radio and I'd have to wait for them both to merge again so my imaginary car band could do our stuff.

Unfortunately the guitarist in the back was hungry.

'Are we stopping here? I really need to eat.'

Bloody musicians.

Jarvis had seen the road sign that told him the last chance to stop before the M5 was coming up in half a mile. I knew where that last chance to stop was and how bad the food tasted.

'Seriously?' I said.

'I'm starving.'

I sighed and overtook one last caravan before settling into the inside lane and pulling the car in to the car park of another former Mister Breakfast roadside restaurant. I parked next to the makeshift sign that said, in plain black lettering: Road Fill.

Road Fill looked like a squat restaurant: like the proprietors weren't paying rent and so might not be planning on staying long. The menus had been handwritten and then photocopied on a photocopier low on ink and the staff's uniforms were the old leftover Mister Breakfast uniforms, with the embroidered logos picked off with a needle. Everywhere you looked there were traces of the previous owners that hadn't been properly removed. There were rectangular patches in the cooking grease on the wallpaper where the Mister Breakfast special offer signs had been removed and the initials 'MB' were still embedded in the side of the table tops and the backs of the chairs. The place hadn't been properly cleaned since it had changed hands. On the toilet door a piece of plastic wife-beater vest was left behind from the snapped off Mister Breakfast sign, and pinned to the toilet wall there was a sheet of A4 paper showing the last time the toilets had been cleaned and who'd cleaned them. It was some considerable time ago. His name was Gary.

There were still specks of blood in the cracks between the skirting board and the wall in the corridor between the toilets and eating area of Road Fill, from where the Breakfast Killer had first struck almost five years ago. That first attack hadn't been fatal. If anything he was just the Breakfast Attacker then. The papers would have to wait with their fingers crossed for a while before they'd get a murder, but the blood still added to the general deathlike ambience of Road Fill.

The funny thing is; the spattered blood, the violent history, the tacky décor, the dirty toilet and the incredibly shoddy service really should have made for a terrible restaurant experience, but no, the food at Road Fill was delicious, worthy of two Michelin stars. No of course it wasn't. Unless you like your fried eggs phlegmy and everything else raw or burned to a crisp, the Road Fill food was even more disgusting than its predecessor's.

In the Road Fill car park I popped the boot of the car and stood in the rain getting wet while I hunted for an umbrella so Jarvis wouldn't end up with wet and curly hair on the short walk to the restaurant. I accumulate umbrellas. There were six in the boot of the car: two retractable black umbrellas, a navy blue one, a dark brown umbrella with an elephant's head for a handle, a broken spotted pink one and a green and white golf umbrella.

'I'm afraid there's only this one,' I said to Jarvis, handing him the broken spotted pink umbrella. As he climbed out of the car, amongst the multicoloured strands of his hair that looked like Play-Doh that had been forced through one of their toy hairdresser gizmos, I saw patches of bare scalp. There was a time when I would have loved to ask Jarvis about it. Going curly in the rain was one thing but the thought that he might one day be bald literally kept Jarvis awake at night. 'All that artificial colouring can't help,' I would have once said, and then I would have told him a horror story about someone I'd seen on the News who'd had their hair dyed and it had all fallen out and they'd ended up looking like Gollum from *Lord of the Rings*. I had a whole box of Christmas cracker jokes I would have loved to have read out to Jarvis in the past when he thought he might be losing his hair: *Why do bald men never go on holiday? Because they've got no hair to go. Why did the bald snooker player have to give up the game? Because the other players kept trying to pot his head.* But not now though. Now that Jarvis actually was going bald it just wasn't that funny any more.

Jarvis jogged across the car park under the pink umbrella and went into Road Fill and straight to the gents, while I waited to be seated in the empty restaurant by the sign that instructed me to do so.

A spotty waiter with the name Sandra sewn into his former Mister Breakfast shirt was watching a daytime talk show on an old TV fixed to the wall near the kitchen. On the TV two big women in tracksuits were shouting, beeping and pointing at each other while the show's presenter and a bouncer tried to keep them apart.

Sandra ignored me and carried on watching the TV, so I went and found my own seat. After about five minutes Jarvis came out of the toilet, where he'd been rearranging the strands of his Play-Doh comb over. If anything, he now looked slightly balder than when he'd gone in. He hung around by a sparsely stocked shelf of chocolate bars, Travel Scrabble games and pocket tissues before coming over and joining me. I asked him what he was looking for over at the counter.

'Nothing,' he said, cutting my question off before I'd finished asking it. We sat in silence for about three days looking at the hand-written menus and occasionally coughing loudly to attract Sandra's attention until he finally dragged himself away from the TV, put his stupid waiter hat on to reluctantly come and take our order. When he got to our table I could see that Sandra's stupid Road Fill waiter's hat was the same stupid Mister Breakfast hat that Jarvis and I used to wear, only with the Mister B logo picked off.

I chose scrambled eggs on toast and coffee from the menu and Jarvis went for the Slaughterhouse Five – sausage, bacon, liver, kidney and black pudding. We had to repeat the order three times, because Sandra was distracted by the TV and kept forgetting to write it down. He took our order over to the cook and went back to watching the daytime talk show. One of the big women had just stormed out of the studio beeping like a trooper. She was swearing so much that the beep machine couldn't keep up with her and a couple of fucks, three shits and half a piss slipped out. On the way out of the studio the swearing fat woman spat at the show's presenter. Daytime talk shows had certainly changed in the past eighteen years or so.

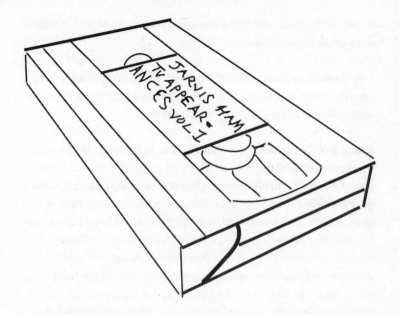

Top of the Morning talk show – ITV – August 8th 1994

TRANSCRIPT

Presenter: *'Thank you. Good morning. Good morning good morning and good morning. Today we're going to be asking the question: is there still a need for a Royal Family?'*

Music

Presenter: *'So, welcome. Should we still be paying for the Royal Family? Have they become obsolete? What value do they bring to modern Britain? Is it time to abolish the monarchy and to become a republic? And if we choose to keep them, aside from the Queen, Prince Phillip and their children, what about the other royals? The* *extended Royal Family? What about Diana? Yes, the blonde lady at the back in the purple blouse?'*

The blonde lady at the back in the purple blouse garbles something about the tourist industry and how very brilliant Diana is. He doesn't correct the presenter about his gender.

BBC Radio Devon *Summer Spectacular* **– Plymouth Hoe – September 4th 1994**
In a short clip recorded from the local TV news we see Jarvis, now with pink streaks in his blonde hair and wearing tartan Bermuda shorts and toy sunglasses with red plastic frames. He's on a stage on the back of a flatbed truck with a BBC Radio Devon balloon wedged between his legs. An audience of holidaymakers and local unemployeds clap along as Jarvis tries to pass the balloon to the next person's waiting legs. The balloon bursts. Everyone cheers. A small crowd of kids appear to be chanting 'Balloon head, balloon head!'

Television South West News **– October 21st 1994**
A report about the closure of Southamleys toyshop following the loss of a court battle with Hamleys in Regent Street over the misuse of the Hamleys logo. It's the second time Southamleys has been in trouble with the law, the news report says. The first time was when a man unsuccessfully sued the store after a member of its staff flew a toy helicopter into his daughter's face. Cut to some old footage of Jarvis Ham dressed as Biggles trying to control a model helicopter, his tongue lolling out of the side of his mouth in concentration as he tries not to crash the helicopter. He looks like a camel doing a Rubik's cube. And then the background action cuts to Jarvis chasing an escaped model helicopter into the shop which almost decapitates a series of ducking customers. As he passes another member of staff

*who is holding a large bunch of helium filled balloons, just for a
moment Jarvis's head completely disappears amongst the balloons.
Like a magic trick.*

The Antiques Roadshow – Britannia Royal Naval College –
Dartmouth – November 20th 1994
*Jarvis is henna red and has a small goatee beard. He is wearing a
pinstriped suit and apparently no shirt. He speaks in a made up
posher than he is voice, like it's 1940 and there's a war on. Jarvis has
brought along an assortment of crockery from the Ham and Hams
Teahouse and the expert looks at all the non matching cups and
saucers laid out on the table for a bit and says, 'If only you had the
full set, I think, for insurance purposes, you would have been looking
at fifty to a hundred thousand pounds. Unfortunately, what you
have here is worth fuck all.'*

Channel Four Racing – Exeter Racecourse – December 1994
*The presenter who is a well-known idiot and figure of ridicule is
standing in front of the grandstand reading out the odds for the next
race and tic-tacking to camera. Behind him Jarvis Ham moves his
fat head from side to side trying to get into the centre of the shot.
Every time Jarvis moves his head into shot the presenter shifts his
position to obscure Jarvis. It's an idiot-and-figure-of-ridicule-off.*

'Do you want sauce?' Sandra said.

The News had started over on the Road Fill TV and the News is
really boring so spotty Sandra took a break to bring us our food. I
asked for some ketchup. It never came.

I poked at my grey microwaved scrambled egg with a fork for a
while and Jarvis tried to get his knife through something that I
think may have ended up on his plate as the result of a nasty fall at
the last fence at the racecourse that was directly opposite us on the

other side of the A38, the scene of the 1994 Idiot-and-Figure-of-Ridicule Championships.

I eventually gave up on my solid pile of warm on the outside and still frozen on the inside scrambled eggs. I put the knife and fork down onto my plate and pushed the plunger on the cafetiere, hoping the restaurant might explode.

Perhaps it was bad food like this that had annoyed someone so much that they attacked the man in the toilet corridor.

It wasn't.

The attack had been unprovoked. The victim was minding his own business – literally – he'd just finished in the toilet and had stepped out into the corridor. He thinks he may have paused for a moment to check his flies were done up, and he'd heard somebody coming out of the toilet behind him. Next thing he knew he was hurtling face first into the corridor wall and then time stopped until he woke in a hospital ward with a policewoman sitting on a chair next to his bed.

He'd been discovered half an hour or so after the attack by a member of staff (not Sandra, Sandra was new); he was unconscious with a broken nose and two missing teeth. His wallet and car keys were still in his pocket. The member of staff hadn't seen anyone else going into the toilet before the attack or coming out after it. The Mister Breakfast staff were not particularly observant: a tradition that had been taken up and carried on at Road Fill as demonstrated for us today by Sandra. The police had very little to go on. They put up a poster appealing for witnesses by the till and left it at that.

The faded poster was still there by the till when we went up to pay. Sandra was ignoring us and watching TV again. The News was finished and there was an advert for yoghurt on. A bunch of attractive women were running down a grassy hill singing about how fantastic the yoghurt was. When they were finished doing that an advert for furniture started. The final clip on *Jarvis Ham TV Appearances Vol. 1* was an advert for furniture.

Television South West – Furniture Circus – Boxing Day 1994
The Furniture Circus Boxing Day Sale advert was only shown once at about three in the morning when advertising rates were at their cheapest. In the ad a culturally diverse and impossibly happy family try out sofas in Furniture Circus's Devon showroom. Nothing to pay till February! a ringmaster shouts and cracks a whip. A woman swings by on a trapeze. A strongman in a striped Victorian bathing suit bends an iron bar into the same shape as his upside down handlebar moustache. A clown on a unicycle juggles between the sofas almost knocking over Jarvis Ham – dressed in a gorilla costume. I don't know why he was dressed as a gorilla. I guess Furniture Circus couldn't afford an elephant.

JARVIS GOES TO LONDON

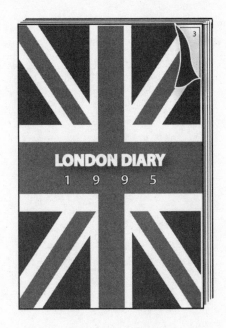

Jarvis Ham's first trip to London since the day he was taken there in his mother's womb was like a montage of the city's top tourist attractions, constructed from stock library footage for a bad American movie where the chisel-chinned and gorgeous hero and his idiotic balloon-faced sidekick take a stock footage flight across the Atlantic to rescue Her Majesty The Queen from a sniper's bullet before recovering the Crown Jewels, going to a casino, putting it all on black, winning a fortune, sleeping with some posh girls and taking a stock footage flight back home again.

All that and an audition for a boyband.

This is a massively abridged version of the sort of thing I had to listen to on the coach all the way back from London to Devon afterwards. It was a relief when Jarvis stopped talking to be sick.

Hold tight.

JUNE 30th 1995

London was brilliant. We went to the Houses of Parliament and set our watches by Big Ben (it's the bell not the clock) and then we watched the changing of the guards at Horse Guards Parade and I had a picture taken with one of the horses. It was gigantic. We then waited at the end of Downing Street but didn't see John Major. I had my photo taken there with a policeman though. After that we climbed on a lion in Trafalgar Square. I got vertigo and had to be helped back down and then we went to Buckingham Palace. All the tourists were staring through the gates but I knew that because the flag wasn't flying the Queen wasn't there. We then sat upstairs on a bus to Madame Tussauds waxworks near Baker Street (I didn't see Sherlock Holmes ha ha). The best waxworks were the Tom Cruise one and both of the wax Dianas, although I didn't think the Diana in her wedding dress looked like her but the other one did. In the more realistic one she was smiling though, so maybe it wasn't so realistic after all. I had my picture taken with Tom Cruise (wax version). One day there will be a Jarvis Ham waxworks in Madame Tussauds. True. Then we went to the British Museum. Forget about wax, they should have a stone Jarvis Ham statue there. And of course one day they will. Probably one hundred or maybe one thousand years after my death. Not yet though. We went to the room with all the Egyptian stuff in. I asked an old looking man who worked there if he remembered me being born there. He said he didn't. I worked out (based on a map Dad drew me) the exact spot in the museum where I was born. I don't know exactly what was there back then but now it's a lot of mummy cases and old bandages and possibly even some dead Egyptians. It must have been like being born in a cemetery. Or an undertakers. I wonder if anyone has ever been born in either of those two places. I suppose they must have. There are a lot of stairs at the British Museum. I didn't count them but I would estimate about three hundred million. We could have used the lifts but I don't like lifts. What if it breaks down? I have claustrophobia. I might be stuck in the lift with someone with even worse claustrophobia. Because of all the stairs I was quite tired when we got to the audition.

THE AUDITION!!

Three people from Entertainment Entertainment (the record company) were sitting at a table and they asked me about my hobbies and my favourite music and what my ambitions were and things like that. They asked me about my dancing and acting skills. I told them about all the acting I'd done (even the gorilla) and I had to fill in a form and sign it three times. On the form I ticked yes in the boxes next to street dancing and break dancing (luckily they didn't ask me to demonstrate, phew!) (Especially after all those stairs at the museum, double phew!!) They always have a member of the band who doesn't do all the dancing anyway. I think that's me. Then I sang all of 'Ice Ice Baby' by Vanilla Ice and half of 'Pray' by Take That. After the audition had finished we had a long time to wait before the coach home. We walked (I've never walked so far in my life as we walked on this one day) down to Oxford Street where some Hare Krishna people were singing and banging drums and I bought one of their books. I left it on the coach home by mistake so I don't know what was in it. Then we went to Piccadilly Circus and saw the neon signs. There were a lot of people there and some of them were a bit scary. One man asked us for money or heroin and a woman who I think was definitely a prostitute asked us if we wanted to go indoors out of the rain with her (it wasn't raining). We ignored her and walked away. There are a lot of mad people in London. And mad birds too. A pigeon nearly flew in my face and nearly gave me the plague. At the coach station there were even more mad people. We had to wait for ever for the coach home. On the coach I was sick because I don't like the smell of the seats on coaches and then the coach broke down and we had to wait for hours outside a Mister Breakfast, which was closed. I've only just got home. I'm going to bed now. I hope I passed the audition. I'm going to try to sleep with my fingers crossed. Is that possible? I could be in a pop band soon. I bet I dream about it. People always tell me I have a great voice and should be a singer. Goodnight (or rather, good morning). Thank you very much (in the style of Elvis).

I think I've lost my voice.

Thank God for that.

Those people who were always telling Jarvis he had a great voice and should be a singer were deaf.

Which made them lucky.

That's him singing in the back of the car now. Don't you think he sounds like an actor playing a character who can't sing and who has to do karaoke for a hilarious scene set in a karaoke bar? He sounds like he's putting it on. Nobody sings like that in real life. I know his voice is out of tune but it seems to be consistently out of tune. He's the same amount of flat on every note. Like a guitar left in front of a window on a sunny day. Like he just needs a tweak.

The audition for 543212345 – the boyband Jarvis was hoping to join – was held in a dusty room at the back of a crumbling church without a congregation on Tottenham Court Road. What that church needed was a funny sign outside. Something like 'Christ on a bike! Christ on a bus, Christ in your car, Christ in your life' or 'A man's best friend is his God', or even one that I once typed out and emailed to a vicar when I was drunk, 'Jesus Loves

You – Even if everyone else thinks you're a cunt'. Okay, maybe not that one.

Like at the *Oliver!* audition Jarvis was the oldest and least talented person in the room and I don't know why they let him sing his Take That song, they'd already heard him rap, surely that was enough to tell them what they needed to know. Perhaps they let him start a second song because it had been a long day and they were bored and thought it was funny, or because they thought they were victims of a wind-up and wanted to see how long Jarvis would keep the act up. Nobody really sings like that, they might have been thinking. This idiot sounds like an actor playing a character who can't sing and who has to do karaoke for a hilarious scene set in a karaoke bar.

Or how about this? Maybe Jarvis had just given them the idea for what would one day become the recognised formula for the first episode of a TV talent show: the one where we all piss ourselves laughing at the freaks, the fat guys, the weirdos and the mentally ill.

Halfway through his destruction of Take That it didn't really matter, because they'd finally had enough. One of the auditioning panel removed his fingers from his ears to raise his hand and stop Jarvis. He actually said 'Don't call us, we'll call you.'

Jarvis was too thick skinned to take the hint. In his balloon head he'd passed the audition. Before the end of the week, with Jarvis as the member of the band who doesn't do all the dancing, 543212345 would have topped the charts, toured and conquered the world, fallen out over musical differences and taken a bit of time out to work on their solo albums. Jarvis had already designed the sleeve for his.

There's a track listing and everything.

He's signed to EMI.

1. Your Majesty
2. Top Gun
3. The Jarvis Ham Rap
4. Helicopter Pilot
5. I Want You
6. Princess
7. Fantasy Lady
8. L is for Love
9. Ice Ice Baby*
10. Princess (instrumental)

All songs written by Jarvis Ham except *Vanilla Ice, Earthquake,
R Brown, J Deacon, F Mercury, M Smooth, D Bowie, R Taylor, B May

Jarvis's debut solo album was in the big brown suitcase. I didn't need to listen to it because it was a CD single of '(Everything I Do) I Do It For You' by Bryan Adams which had been number one in the pop charts for sixteen thousand weeks in 1991 and I'd already heard it. A couple of weeks after the boyband audition Entertainment Entertainment still hadn't called Jarvis, so ignoring their strict instructions to not call them, he called them.

JULY 17th 1995

Telephoned Entertainment Entertainment today. There was no answer. I will try again tomorrow.

JULY 18th 1995

Phoned Entertainment Entertainment and got through to their answer phone. I didn't leave a message. I panicked a bit if I'm honest.

JULY 20th 1995

Telephoned Entertainment Entertainment twice today and left a message on their answer phone the second time I phoned.

JULY 22nd 1995

In Plymouth HMV my solo records will be filed in between Hall & Oates and Happy Mondays.

JULY 24th 1995

Tried telephoning Entertainment Entertainment again (three times!) ((Didn't leave a message))

JULY 27th 1995

Telephoned Entertainment Entertainment. There was no answer and no answer phone.

JULY 28th 1995

Spoke to a lady at Entertainment Entertainment today. She said she didn't know if a decision had been made yet and if they said to not call them because they'd call me then maybe that was what I should do. She was a bit rude if I'm honest.

JULY 29th 1995

Charles and Diana's fourteenth wedding anniversary today. The tradition for the fourteenth anniversary is for the husband to buy his wife something made from ivory. I don't think Charles will have bothered. Entertainment Entertainment still haven't rung.

JULY 31st 1995

Dad says that no news is good news.

AUGUST 1st 1995

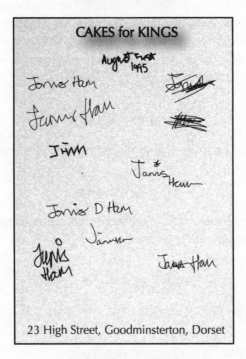

AUGUST 2nd 1995

Entertainment Entertainment still haven't rung. Maybe Dad is wrong about no news being good news. He isn't a show business expert as far as I can remember.

AUGUST 4th 1995

A man vomited his cream tea up today. His wife started screaming, 'He's dead! He's dead! He's dead! He's dead! David is dead!' (I made the name David up but she did scream that he was dead a lot). Dad called an ambulance and they took David (not his real name) to the hospital with an oxygen mask on. It was like an episode from *Casualty*. Dad was worried the other customers would think the cream was poisoned or past its sell by date and he gave everyone free cups of tea. Mum was in bed (ill) and slept through it all.

AUGUST 7th 1995

I think that *some* news would definitely be better news.

AUGUST 9th 1995

I rang Entertainment Entertainment again today. The rude lady said to try again tomorrow.

AUGUST 10th 1995

No answer at Entertainment Entertainment all day.

AUGUST 11th 1995

I spoke to a man at Entertainment Entertainment. He said all the members of 543212345 had been chosen six months ago. Four months before the audition. I don't understand.

AUGUST 14th 1995

I was really upset yesterday but I've now realised I was actually quite lucky. And it's not just me that thinks so. Everyone says that being in a boyband would have been a big career mistake for me and everyone also says that the time for boybands has been and gone and 543212345 have missed the boat and they will never ever be famous or successful.

TOP 40 SINGLES
Week commencing 1st October 1995

1	(-)	543212345	Jump Jump Jump	Entertainment Entertainment
2	(1)	Wet Wet Wet	Love is All Around	London Records
3	(7)	Kylie Minogue	Confide in Me	Deconstruction

'Jump Jump Jump' was the fastest-selling debut single of all time. It stayed at the top of the charts right up until Christmas. The band performed it on the *Christmas Top of the Pops* as a special Christmas present for Jarvis. To wish him a Happy New Year they sang it for him on Jools Holland's New Year's Eve *Hootenanny* show accompanied by Jools on the piano. And it carried on like that for a while. 543212345 rubbing it in with a number one album, 543212345 with another number one single, 543212345 winning three BRIT Awards, 543212345 singing the official *Children's Dreams Come True* single, 543212345 meeting the Queen, 543212345 meeting Diana!, 543212345 advertising corn flakes, 543212345 dolls, 543212345 hats, *543212345 the Movie*.

'Change the station! Change the station!' And 543212345 reformed and more successful than ever, playing on my car radio seventeen years later. Jarvis put his sausage fingers in his cauliflower ears and went 'Wmmmm wmmmm wmmmm' until I retuned the radio. At least it stopped him singing along with it. I had seriously been considering crossing the central reservation and driving into the speeding southbound traffic to shut him up.

When we'd left Road Fill the rain had stopped. Just as well, because Jarvis had left my girlfriend's spotty pink umbrella under the seat in the restaurant. That would give her another fifteen minutes of material for when I got home.

As we exited the A38 to join the M5 we passed the former Mister Breakfast over on the southbound side of the road. It was the one where the coach had broken down on the way back home after the 543212345 audition. It's a diner now. There's a neon sign on the roof that flashes the word 'DINER' on and off at night. Before it changed hands it was the scene of the second Mister Breakfast attack.

The second attack took place in the car park out the back. There were security cameras but they weren't switched on. As with the first attack, there was no apparent motive. Both victims had been white males between the ages of twenty-five and forty who were driving home when they stopped for something to eat or drink and to use the toilets.

A weapon was used in the second attack. It was a blunt object; the police said at the press conference, it was probably a large spanner or a monkey wrench. Aren't they both the same thing? a newspaper reporter asked the police. It was possible the attacker was a plumber or a car mechanic the police suggested.

It wasn't noticed at first, perhaps because it was so obvious, but both attacks had taken place on the same day, one year apart.

I checked the rear-view mirror to see how my passenger was doing. He was sulking. It was 543212345's fault. The idiots. Jarvis could sulk for England. If somebody with such a round head could ever be referred to as having a long face, this was that time. I think a good hard sulk gave him pleasure.

To avoid making eye contact with my reflection in the mirror and risk breaking his world championship sulk Jarvis squashed his face against the car window. He stared down into the man-made valley beneath the motorway and the vast holiday park of static holiday homes and retirement chalets below.

As we drove over the holiday and retirement park Jarvis would have been able to see the man-made lake and its fleet of yachts – looking like toy sailboats in a big bath. He would have seen tiny OAPs and holidaymakers playing tennis on the tennis courts or crown bowls on the artificially grassed bowling green. There was also a heated swimming pool, a giant chess set, a nine-hole golf course and a bingo night the first Thursday of every month.

Jarvis's parents owned a two-bedroom static home in the Golden Parachutes Holiday and Retirement Village. Jarvis's dad had bought it so that his wife would have somewhere to escape to whenever she needed a break without having to travel too far.

Jarvis's mum would never be strong enough to ever really take advantage of all the Golden Parachutes' wonderful facilities. She never made it to the bingo, didn't know the rules of chess and suffered too much from sea sickness to ever go out in a yacht, and although the holiday and retirement park was surrounded by miles of glorious Devon countryside, Mrs Ham was never well enough to take a long walk through any of it.

I took another look at Jarvis who now seemed to be attempting to actually force his sulking face through the glass of the window. His sulk was about to go nuclear. I needed something to snap him out of it.

'Car game?' I said.

Jarvis didn't pause to think about it for a second as he pulled his face away from the glass, leaving a sweaty cheek stain behind.

'I went into a shop and bought an apple,' he said.

'I went into a shop and bought an apple and a banana.'

'I went into a shop and bought an apple, a banana and a clarinet.'

'I went into a shop and bought an apple, a banana, a clarinet and a diplodocus.'

'A diplodocus? What kind of shop is this?'

'A diplodocus, clarinet and fruit shop.'

'Good shop.'

'Come on, your turn.'

'Right. I went into a shop and bought an apple, a banana,' Jarvis was recounting the objects incredibly fast now. 'A clarinet, a diplodocus and Elvis.'

'I went into a shop and bought an apple, a banana … what was it … don't tell me … a clarinet, a diplodocus, Elvis and … Five.'

'Five what?'

'Five … four,3212345.'

'Oh ha *ha ha*.'

'Come on.'

'I went into a shop and bought an apple, a banana, a clarinet, a diplodocus, Elvis, 543212345 and a gun to shoot them with.'

You get the idea.

Z was a zebra.

Z was always a zebra.

In the summer of 1996 Jarvis went brunette. He hadn't had much fun as a blonde. That was a myth.

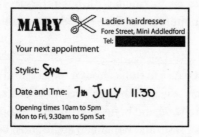

Sue was the stylist in *Mary* that day.

Sue was new. She was half the age of all the other women working at *Mary*. And like every other female that he was attracted to, Jarvis thought Sue looked like Princess Diana. She didn't.

If I was unkind and if it helps to make all of this a bit funnier I'd say Sue looked more like Prince Charles.

She didn't.

But she did have big ears.

* * *

Sue was a good swimmer. I don't know if the ears helped at all with that, probably not, I've never seen a big-eared fish. She was broad shouldered too. And I don't know what came first there either: the broad shoulders or the good swimming. Anyway, Sue went to the pool two or three times a week and swam in the sea in all weathers. She'd been on the front page of the local papers receiving a medal from some celebrity or other after she'd dived in to an icy river to save a child who'd fallen in. Way to go Sue.

During one of her hairdresser to client conversations Sue looked at Jarvis in the large hairdressing mirror, his hair was wrapped in tin foil and a trickle of purple dye had started to run down the edge of his forehead. Sue dabbed it with a wet flannel and said, 'You should come swimming.'

Oh Sue. Sue, Sue, Sue. Why couldn't you have asked him if he was going anywhere nice for his holidays or whether he wanted anything for the weekend? Where's your sense of tradition Sue? What are they teaching at Hairdressing College these days?

Come on Sue. You do the math.

A girl who looks like Princess Diana + the opportunity to see her in her swimming costume – the fact that Jarvis can't swim = that rather handsome waiter from the Mister Breakfast earlier having to teach him how.

And the chlorine was going to ruin Jarvis's hair.

JARVIS LEARNS TO SWIM

Why couldn't Sue teach Jarvis how to swim if she was supposed to be so good at it? She would have loved it. Lots of swimming involved. Sue would have known what to do at that first swimming lesson when her pupil stood on the changing room side of the pre-swim showers and mini paddling pool, trembling in his stars and stripes trunks and denouncing his hydrophobia, 'It's not a fear of water!' He shouted at me so loudly that a tiny child nearby started crying. 'It's a fear of *DROWNING! A FEAR OF DROWNING!*' Seriously Sue, you would have loved it. And there was shopping involved as well. Women love shopping.

20 8 96

SWIMMING essentials

trunks (2 pairs)
goggles
towels (2)
earplugs
noseclip
armbands (inflatable)
shampoo etc
Bag
towelling dressing gown
swimming hat
flip-flops (verrucas)
shaver gel
T.Brush

Clipping his nose and plugging his ears wasn't going to be enough to get Jarvis in the water. He didn't need flip-flops and shower gel: he needed hypnosis. And a *dressing gown*? Who did Jarvis think he was? Noel Coward? Maybe it was to go with his pyjamas for when he eventually earned his lifesaving certificate, diving in to the deep end to rescue a rubber brick.

Also …

1. How old do you have to be before you're too old to wear inflatable swimming armbands?
2. How unfit are you if you're so out of breath after blowing one of the armbands up that you have to lie down in the changing room for ten minutes to stop yourself from throwing up?

And finally:

3. Surely Jarvis's big balloon head would have been the only buoyancy aid he'd need.

MY (JARVIS D HAM) SWIMMING JOURNAL

AUGUST 22nd 1996

I'm learning to swim. I need to learn as quickly as possible so I can go to the beach or the swimming baths with Sue. She works at MARY. Sue is a really brilliant swimmer. Also, not only does she look like Diana

She didn't.

but she saved someone from drowning once, which is exactly what Diana did last year when a man fell in a pond in Regents Park in London. Wow.

AUGUST 23rd 1996

First swimming lesson today and it was a disaster. Totally. 100%. I feel like giving up. ~~Bloody hell~~.

AUGUST 26th 1996

I nearly drowned today! That isn't a lie.

AUGUST 28th 1996

Charles and Diana got divorced today. The man on TV said Diana would be getting thirty million dollars. I don't know if that means she is moving to America. I do hope not. I think she should be allowed to get on with her life now. Two days till swimming. I can't wait (lie).

AUGUST 30th 1996

Stupid swimming. Stupid swimming. Stupid swimming. Stupid swimming. Stupid swimming. Stupid swimming. Stupid swimming. Stupid swimming. Stupid swimming. Stupid swimming. Stupid swimming.

SEPTEMBER 2nd 1996

That same group of girls were at the pool today. I hate them.
They splashed me and called me names. Stupid names. I
can't even write some of them down because they're so
horrible. The biggest one (the leader) tried to trip me up. I
could have been seriously injured. I called her a fat cow and
it was me who was told off by the lifeguard!! Why weren't
they at school? (The girls not the lifeguards.)

SEPTEMBER 6th 1996

Overall it was a more successful lesson today. I went in the
water ~~at least~~ at last. Ha ha ha.

Once I'd got Jarvis to actually put his feet into the water it was then
simply a case of getting him to climb down all four steps of the
short ladder that led down into the shallow end and put both his
feet on the floor of the pool and get the rest of his body wet too.
Then all I had to do was convince him it was safe to let go of the
ladder and then to let go of the bar that ran along the side of the
pool, to put his face in the water, to stop moaning about how cold
the water was and how the chlorine made his eyes sting and how it
was going to make his hair go green, basically to just shut the fuck
up and get on with the swimming already.

SEPTEMBER 9th 1996

I think it will take a lot longer to learn to swim than I thought
at first. Why is it taking so long? Why didn't my parents teach
me when I was younger? Why?

I've got a reasonably good idea.

SEPTEMBER 20th 1996

I properly swam today. Properly. I did the front crawl with both feet off the ground. It was brilliant. I think I'm going to be a natural swimmer.

JARVIS HAM'S TOP TEN MOTIVATIONAL SWIMMING SONGS

'Wannabe' – The Spice Girls
'Ooh Aah … Just a Little Bit' – Gina G
'Ice Ice Baby' – Vanilla Ice
'Firestarter' – The Prodigy
'Spaceman' – Babylon Zoo
'Earth Song' – Michael Jackson (The King of Pop)
'Return of the Mack' – Mark Morrison
'We Will Rock You' – Queen
'Go West' – Pet Shop Boys
'Country House' – Blur

SEPTEMBER 27th 1996

At work today I had aches and pains all over my body. I felt like I'd fallen down a very very steep flight of stairs onto a bumpy road where I was run over by a steamroller, two tractors and a lorry. Full of bricks. And lead. And an anvil. I'm not exaggerating.

Jarvis's early lack of confidence in the water soon turned into over-confidence and he started to show off. At the pool there were three swimming lanes: a slow lane, a medium lane and a fast lane. Although Jarvis was too slow for the slow lane he would insist on going in the fast lane and annoying all the serious swimmers who'd be stuck in a gridlock behind him. What he really needed was his own lane. A Jarvis Lane.

And there was the time when he first jumped into the water rather than climbing down the short ladder, and I swear to God he bounced along the surface – like in *The Dambusters*.

Twice a week for three hundred and fifty years I had to get up when it was still dark at fifteen-minutes-to-stupid to go swimming with Jarvis.

I had to watch him crowbar his jelly baby of a body into his Old Glory Speedos. I'd have to wait while he meticulously folded his clothes like he was making origami swans and put them in one of the changing room lockers. I'd have to lend him a twenty pence piece to get the key out of the lock – Jarvis never had his own 20p, he never had any money on him, ever. Every time we go anywhere he always says that he needs to go to the cashpoint first and it has to be the cashpoint in the wall of 123 Fore Street as it's the only one he trusts – everyone is out to steal Jarvis Ham's identity for some reason. His PIN number is 1234 by the way. Feel free. He's all yours.

Once his clothes were in the locker he'd put his flip-flops on and flip-flop to the toilet, even if he didn't really need to go. He then put the plugs in his ears and the clip on his nose and waste a considerable amount of time in front of the mirror doing his hair before folding it all up into a tight rubber hat. He'd then put his goggles on and flip-flop towards the pool.

Jarvis couldn't see a thing without his glasses – he said everyone looked like they were being reflected in a dirty train window – and he had to feel his way, holding onto the walls like he was on his way to the duty free shop on a cross Channel ferry in a storm.

Out of the water, with his glasses off and goggles on, his ears plugged and his nose clipped, Jarvis looked a bit like a synchronized swimmer, the exact opposite of what he actually was when he was in the water – flapping about and causing the lifeguards to move forward onto the edge of their high chairs, ready to dive in and save somebody – or possibly a dog – who was drowning.

'I swallowed so much water today,' Jarvis would say, coughing and spluttering, bent over with his hands on his knees after a particularly traumatic swim. 'What if I catch something?'

'The urine will have killed off anything infectious,' I'd reassure him.

When Jarvis was finished getting dried and dressed after his swim it was like a bath bomb had gone off at Kew Gardens. A fog of talcum powder filled the changing room, a real sweet pea-souper. The showers would be full of shampoo and conditioner bubbles for a week. The whole building would smell like one of those LUSH handmade soap shops. And then I'd be late for work while I waited for him to finish drying his ridiculous hair.

I found this picture in the shoebox:

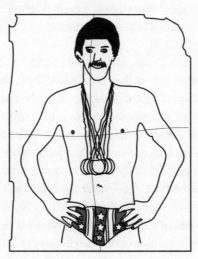

Jarvis had the trunks. The medals and the moustache would come later I imagine.

DECEMBER 3rd 1996

There was red, white and blue bunting hanging over the pool today. There'd been a swimming gala at the weekend. The bunting reminded me of Diana and thinking of her seemed to make me swim better. I'm getting very good at it. I had swum nearly a whole length without stopping. And then I thought I was dreaming because I thought I could actually see Diana sitting on the edge of the pool up at the deep end. I knew it couldn't possibly be her though, and as I swam a bit nearer I thought that it was actually Jennifer Fer, which made me panic. I was already out of breath from nearly swimming a whole length without stopping. And I swallowed some water and my goggles steamed up and I had to go to the side of the pool to cough for a while. I took my goggles off and looked to see if it was Jennifer Fer but I couldn't see properly without my glasses.

I could see. It wasn't Diana, nor was it Jennifer Fer. I could see her. Down at the other end of the pool, past Jarvis thrashing about like he was auditioning for a part in *Jaws,* with a mouthful of chlorinated water and pensioner piss, his rubber-hatted head bobbing about in the water like a lost beach ball. I could see. I saw her. Down past the lifeguard who was gently lowering an old lady into the water on the pensioner ducking stool that was basically an orange plastic office chair with the legs removed and badly welded to a crude winch. Past all that, I could see her. As 543212345 boomed derisively in from the water aerobics class in the training pool next door and reverberated off the tiled walls, I saw her, and eventually so could Jarvis. Not Diana and not Jennifer Fer, but Sue, the jug-eared freakily shouldered hairdressing woman of Jarvis's recent dreams. Sue – ignoring all the no petting signs as she French kissed an Italian lifeguard down at the deep end of the pool.

We're on the A30 now. What can I tell you about the A30? 284 miles of road that starts in the centre of London and finishes, inevitably, at Land's End. Historically it's known as the Great South West Road. John Betjeman immortalised it in his poem 'Meditation on the A30.' We've just passed Fairmile on the section of A30 where the eco-warrior Swampy famously spent a week in a tunnel to protest at the damage caused to the environment by construction of the road. Jarvis hates getting dirty and doesn't like confined spaces, but if the entrance could have been widened to fit his fat head he would have gladly lived in a tunnel for a week if it would have made him half as famous as Swampy was.

Our most recent car game had lasted not far beyond the short five-mile stretch of the M5 motorway. It was a waste of a car game. Motorways weren't the right place for car games. The speed of the other cars passing us, the lane changing and the fear of an impending pile up would have kept Jarvis distracted on the motorway. Jarvis hated motorways. When he'd gone to the shop and bought a purple poodle he'd done it with his hands over his eyes as we drove up the middle lane and were almost crushed between two bread lorries – a Jarvis Ham sandwich. With me as the mustard.

I'd been such a fool. I went into a Shop and bought an Apple was an A or B road game not a motorway game. Jarvis would be bored again soon and I'd have to think of new ways to keep him distracted: games like Twenty Questions and Have I Got a Moustache? and I hated those games. I could keep Jarvis distracted for a bit by pointing at fields full of cows or pigs, or if I was really lucky, a couple of horses having sex. A boy racer shot by, almost taking my wing mirror with him, and as the A30 merged effortlessly into the A303 I thought about the worst day of Jarvis Ham's life.

AUGUST 31ST 1997

He was serving an early Sunday morning cream tea to an elderly couple from Bristol when he heard the news. The Bristol couple were the first customers of the day. If Jarvis's father had been there with Jarvis he would have heard the news by now and broken it to his son. But Jarvis's father hadn't listened to the news on the radio that morning because his wife was feeling poorly and he'd been busy making her comfortable; reassuring her that there was no need for her to get out of bed and that he and Jarvis would be fine opening the shop and serving the day's customers without her.

While his father fluffed up an extra pillow to help ease the pain in his wife's back Jarvis opened the Ham and Hams Teahouse. The door was barely unlocked when the little bell above it tinkled and the couple from Bristol walked in. It was the last day of their holiday and they'd vowed to return to the Ham and Hams before they drove back to Bristol, for what the man told Jarvis was, 'without a doubt the most delicious cream tea we have ever tasted. You should put a sign in the window saying so,' he said.

Jarvis nodded, took their order and went behind the counter to prepare it. He warmed the scones and put the cream and the jams and the cutlery on a tray. He brewed a pot of tea and put two cups and saucers that weren't made to be together on the tray. He put a small bowl with four separate compartments filled with four different types of sugar – both perfect white cubes and randomly shaped brown chunks. Jarvis put teaspoons on the saucers and a tiny vase of water with a yellow flower in it onto the tray.

When the scones were ready Jarvis put them on warmed plates, he put the plates on the tray and took it all over to the table where the couple from Bristol were sitting. The man was reading a newspaper.

'Such awful news,' the woman said to Jarvis.

Jarvis agreed, presuming it to be more small talk between customer and waiter and that she was right of course, the news did seem to always be awful.

'So young,' the woman said. She looked to Jarvis as though she might cry. 'She can't have been that much older than you. So sad.'

The man nodded in agreement, sighed, looked at the tray and the scones and the jams and cream. He licked his lips, folded his newspaper and placed it on the table where Jarvis saw the first two words of the headline on the front page and fainted.

SEPTEMBER 1st 1997

I've been to the train toilet twice. Once to be sick and the other time because I thought I was going to cry. I've read all the horrible facts now. I'm going to copy them out of the newspaper for something to do. To stop me from crying. I've bought a notebook from Smiths. The train is horrible. A baby keeps crying and screaming. It's as though the baby knows.

SEPTEMBER 1st 1997

The horrible facts copied from the newspaper: at 12.20am
Princess Diana left the Ritz Hotel in Paris in a black Mercedes
car. They were followed by paparazzi photographers on
motorbikes. They drove very fast into a tunnel under the
Place de l'Alma in the centre of Paris. In the tunnel the
Mercedes crashed into a pillar. Diana was rushed to hospital
where surgeons tried to save her. She died at 3am. The paper
says hundreds of mourners have already gathered at
Kensington Palace and laid flowers and teddy bears at the
gates.

SEPTEMBER 1st 1997

There was a stall at Paddington Station that sold Paddington
bears. I bought one and left it at the gates to the palace. I
don't know why people leave teddy bears. It doesn't matter.
It doesn't matter. Nothing matters.

SEPTEMBER 1st 1997

I'm on the train back home now. While I was in London Dad
was going to open the teahouse. He said it would be best to
carry on with business as usual. How can business be as
usual? Dad said that it's terrible but life has to go on. He's
wrong. How can life just go on? I can't be expected to pour
cups of tea like nothing has happened. If he opens again
tomorrow I won't go in. I can't. In the old days people would
wear black for six months or two years or even for ever. In
other countries they pull their hair out or stop washing and
shaving. I wish I lived in a different country or in the old days.

SEPTEMBER 2nd 1997

There are so many horrible things in the newspapers today. There are some nice things as well but too many horrible ones. I don't want to read any of them but can't seem to stop myself. It's like I'm one of those women pulling my hair out. I didn't go into work. I can't. I don't think it was busy in the teahouse anyway. I think everybody is too upset to eat cakes.

The diary of Jarvis's mourning goes on for quite a while. It's not a fun read. There are no witty asides in brackets, no ha ha has, no top tens, nothing is brilliant. The entry for September 3rd is almost illegible. The words are difficult to make out and the pages are wrinkled and the ink has run, possibly with tears, some of it reads like it was written while Jarvis was on a log flume.

On September 5th Jarvis takes the train to Paddington again. Another – presumably different – baby cries for the whole journey and the toilet breaks down somewhere near Taunton. Jarvis spends the rest of the time between Taunton and Paddington trying not to wet himself. Then there's something about a sandwich that's been crossed out.

In London he queues for six hours at St James's Palace to sign the book of condolence – he doesn't say what it was he wrote there. In the queue he talks to people from America and Spain and either a bland lady or a blonde lady, I think it must be a blonde lady, who's either hitched or hatched all the way from Aberdeen.

Jarvis camps the night with no tent or sleeping bag behind the barriers on Whitehall. He says he can see Downing Street. He mentions the time he was there two years before when he had his photo taken with a policeman and how he never wants to have his photograph taken ever again, as he will never smile again. Someone gives him a candle and he keeps it lit for the whole night. He says the people there are sad but there is also a great atmosphere and sometimes it is like a sleepover. There's some stuff that is impossible to read after that and then it's the morning. People are listening to the funeral procession starting on the radio and then everyone is crying. Then people switch their radios off and the whole world is silent apart from the hooves of the horses pulling the carriage and the feet of the soldiers marching slowly past. The last bit on this page of the WH Smith's notepad is almost completely tear stains and ink blots but I'm pretty sure Jarvis is saying that it's the second time he's stood behind a barrier to watch Diana pass by and that his heart is broken.

When Jarvis was queuing to sign the book of condolence he was interviewed for the TV news. He was asked what Diana meant to him and Jarvis told the news reporter how much he would miss her and that he hadn't realised that until it was too late. He talked about how he'd met her in Exeter and she was so warm and friendly and beautiful. It was Jarvis's greatest ever TV performance but I doubt even a fame junkie so into his drug as Jarvis would have been pleased at the way he'd finally made it into the nation's living rooms. It was a shit silver lining.

On September 10th, as the flowers at Kensington Gardens were nearly five feet deep and the bottom layer of flowers was turning into compost, Jarvis's dad asked me if I'd come and talk to his son. He was worried about him.

His dad had told me that Jarvis had stopped shaving and hadn't washed his hair since August. Jarvis hadn't been looking in the newspaper for auditions. He wasn't doing any of his vocal warm ups or writing fantasy acting CVs. He was hardly eating. He wasn't brushing his teeth. He just stayed in bed for as much of the day as he could, like John without a Yoko. His bedroom had started to smell like somebody had died in it.

Jarvis's dad would bring his son the newspapers from the Ham and Hams at the end of the day and Jarvis would take out the special ten and twenty page Diana sections and read them all. He watched the experts and bandwagon jumping ghouls on television with their conspiracy theories, speculating on who was responsible for the tragedy and talking about what it would all mean for the future of the Royal Family. Jarvis watched and read it all and he hated everything that everyone had to say. Everyone had an opinion on what really happened that awful night in Paris. Jarvis believed all of them as much as he didn't believe any of them.

When I came round after work the flag outside the Ham and Hams was the same flag that had been flying there for the past two weeks. Jarvis's dad had been too busy running the Ham and Hams and looking after his ill wife to change it and the brilliant white map of Antarctica at the centre of the sea blue flag had started to turn a not-so-brilliant dirty grey.

I went up to Jarvis's room. He was in bed watching the TV news with the sound down. I put the day's newspapers on his bed.

'People have been stealing teddy bears from Kensington Palace,' Jarvis said. 'Why would anyone do that?'

I shook my head. I didn't know.

'I left a Paddington Bear there. I bought it at the station. They've got a stall there that sells all Paddington Bear stuff. I bought a bear and left it there. At the palace gates. Do you think it's been stolen? I hope it hasn't been stolen. Do you think it's been stolen?'

'I don't know Jarvis. You know your dad is worried about you?'

Jarvis ignored me and continued staring at the silent TV.

'You should go and help your dad. He's exhausted. Running the teahouse and looking after your mum as well.'

'It's too soon. I can't. Not yet ... It's just ... why would someone steal a teddy bear?'

I was out of my depth. I didn't know what to say. I was useless. In the awkward silence of Jarvis's stinky bedroom I considered my options. I came up with five.

1. Slap him across the face screaming, 'Snap out of it!'
2. Give him a hug until he cried it all out.
3. Turn the TV up.
4. Turn the TV off.
5. Leave.

A week after I'd left, Jarvis agreed to return to work: on the conditions that his dad would let him wear a black armband and that Jarvis could open the Ham and Hams Teahouse's own book of condolence on the counter next to the big old Kerching! style till. In return Jarvis agreed to wash his hair, brush his teeth, have a bath and shave.

SIMON AVETON

The red rooftop of the Mister Breakfast revealed itself on the brow of the hill as we came up out of the other side of a rollercoaster like dip in the A303. It looked like the roof of a gingerbread house or a dolls house, or a haunted house, a building on a film set or a model copied and built from a child's drawing. What I'm trying to say is that it didn't look real. A mirage on the A303. An oasis of watered down fizzy soft drinks, weak coffee and warmed up microwave meals for the weary traveller. The closer we got to it I could see there were gaps in the roof where tiles had fallen off. The windows were boarded up and on the door there was a sign that said KEEP OUT.

The child whose drawing this house had been based on needed to see the school nurse.

The rear of the restaurant was just a pile of rubble on the ground. A bulldozer was parked next to it, ready to resume work in the morning. In a few days the rest of the building would be rubble too. In a month the rubble would be cleared away and a month or two after that an exhaust and gearbox replacement centre would take its place. Not long after that – and if it hadn't have been for the Breakfast Killer – nobody would have remembered the red roofed and haunted gingerbread dolls house on the brow of the hill had ever existed.

* * *

As we approached the boarded up roadside restaurant we drove past an ironic or simply unfortunate sign that read TIREDNESS CAN KILL, TAKE A BREAK. Simon Aveton would have seen the sign shortly before he stopped at the Mister Breakfast for coffee and to splash some cold water on his face in the toilets.

His long journey had begun when he'd said goodbye to his wife and son two days earlier. He'd kissed his wife on the lips and his son on the top of his head. How tall he'd grown all of a sudden. Simon Aveton told his wife they must remember to compare their son's height against the pencil marks on the doorframe of his bedroom when he returned from his trip. Which reminded Simon that on his return he also really needed to find the time to redecorate his son's bedroom: he was growing out of the farm animal pictures on the wallpaper, it was time for some trains or drawings of footballers mid-kick.

Simon Aveton kissed his wife and son goodbye, he stroked the cat – who they'd amusingly named David because it didn't sound like a cat's name – and he picked up a black bag of rubbish to drop in the dustbin by the front gate on the way to his shiny new silver Ford Mondeo, before setting off to St Austell to visit his parents and his little sister who wasn't so little any more. Simon Aveton hadn't seen his mum and dad and his little sister anywhere near as often as he'd promised he would when he'd moved away from Cornwall to start his own family in London. They spoke on the phone and he sent his sister emails, but less and less so with each passing year apart. He'd just been so busy.

Simon drove to St Austell and spent some quality time with his old family. They talked about growing up in Cornwall, looked through old photo albums and unfolded the enormous sheet of paper with the Aveton family tree on that Simon's father had spent almost two years researching.

Then Simon Aveton said goodbye, kissed his mother and sister on the cheek and shook hands with his father, and just as he started to feel settled and at home once more it was time to set off on the long drive back to his new family: to measure his son's height against the doorframe and to strip off the sheep and pig wallpaper and put up that big boy wallpaper with the trains or the footballers on.

It was already getting dark when Simon Aveton set off from his parents' house. By the time he reached the A303 he would have dipped his lights to avoid blinding the drivers on the other side of the road over fifty times, with many of the drivers opposite not reciprocating the gesture. They were probably Londoners driving down to their holiday homes, Simon Aveton might have thought to himself. Perhaps one day he'd like to move back down to the old country with his wife and son. Take weekend walks on the beach and get his son into a school without metal detectors at the entrance gates. They could stand outside at night and look up at the stars. Simon had forgotten quite how many stars there were. He'd stood in the garden the night before with his own father and looked up at the sky and had been totally taken aback by the sheer volume of stars he could see. It was like being at the Planetarium. Simon couldn't remember the last time he'd seen more than one star in the light-polluted smog over his London home. He saw more police helicopter lights than he ever saw stars. When he was a child, Simon knew all the names of the constellations and clusters and the patterns they formed in the sky. He remembered some of the names: the Great Bear and the Plough or was it the Big Dipper, and the Frying Pan? But he'd forgotten what they looked like or where to find them in the sky.

Simon Aveton wanted his son to see the star-filled sky – he'd rung his wife to tell her that before he started out on his long drive home. He'd told her that maybe they should think about moving down to Cornwall.

But Simon Aveton knew he had a great job in London and both his wife and son had their friends there. Perhaps he could save up enough to buy a second home in Cornwall. It would be hypocritical after all the slightly drunken speeches he'd made about 'middle class Londoners stealing the homes from the real Cornish people', but family came before values, everyone knew that.

He'd only been away two days and Simon Aveton was already missing his wife and son. What he really needed right now was to get back home to them – he might even get in while his wife was still awake. She'd be waiting up for him anyway, unable to get to sleep while she was thinking about him driving all that way alone in the dark. She'd made him a mix tape for the journey – all the music they both loved – and every couple of tracks his wife had put in a song that she knew would make her husband sing along, it would help him stay awake.

Simon Aveton would have listened to the mix tape three or four times already by the time he passed by the sign telling him that tiredness killed, and maybe he took the sign's advice to take a break.

Simon Aveton would have seen the lights of the Mister Breakfast and seconds later would have pulled into the car park at the side of the building. The car park was empty but he still parked as far away as possible from the entrance to the restaurant. The Mondeo was new and he didn't want somebody parking badly next to him and scratching the paintwork or knocking his wing mirrors off. It was darkest in that part of the car park, the nearest light needed a new bulb but times were not good at Mister Breakfast. The company was in financial trouble. Mister Breakfast simply didn't have the money for new light bulbs. They'd already closed down most of their adjoining budget hotels and were starting to sell off some of their restaurants as well. Mister Breakfast's days were numbered. All this violence wasn't helping either. It turns out all publicity is not good publicity after all.

The CCTV cameras outside the Mister Breakfast were switched off to save money too, so nobody saw Simon Aveton park his silver

Ford Mondeo and nobody – including probably Simon Aveton himself – saw someone come up behind him as he was locking the car door and hit him once and then once again across the back of the head.

The police said that Simon Aveton probably lay unconscious and dying in the car park for an hour or more. It's thought the first blow to the head would have knocked him instantly unconscious and the second would have caused an acute subdural haematoma, a traumatic brain injury involving bleeding inside the skull, which eventually led to Simon Aveton's death. The police taped the area around the crime off for a while and did a fingertip search for a murder weapon. They found nothing. Just used condoms and dog mess.

Once again there seemed to be no obvious motive for the crime. Nothing was stolen. There was nothing sexual or particularly weird about it. No ripping or strangling for the papers to really get the horn over. Nobody got eaten. What a rubbish murder. Nobody did anything properly any more. It was just another act of random and pointless violence. One more badly painted sign of the times.

Three attacks on the same day three years apart was at least enough for a Venn diagram though. And the newspapers were happy because they had their murder. Just like when Jarvis was promoted from Master Breakfast to Mister Breakfast and was allowed to fry eggs, the papers promoted the Breakfast Attacker to the Breakfast Killer.

JARVIS REINVENTS HIMSELF

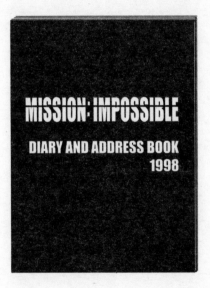

By Christmas of 1997 Jarvis's period of mourning had subsided somewhat. He still talked about Diana all the time and he bought everyone copies of 'Candle in the Wind 1997' for Christmas presents. He rang me up in the middle of the night once to tell me how the UK suicide rate had gone up by seventeen per cent and self-harm had gone up by forty-three per cent in the four weeks after Diana's death. The suicide rate for women who most identified with Diana, Jarvis told me – the women in the same age group as Diana – had gone up by forty-five per cent. He sounded almost envious of them. But for the most part Jarvis seemed to have moved on.

When the Ham and Hams opened up again after the Christmas holidays Jarvis agreed to stop wearing the black armband and he removed the book of condolence from the counter. His father replaced it with a large Panettone.

With no idea that I'd one day be reading it I bought Jarvis a diary for Christmas. It came with a set of four Tom Cruise stickers and on the inside page I wrote *Happy Christmas Jarvis. Use this for all your acting engagements. This diary will self-destruct in five seconds.* If only it had.

No, I take that back. A lot of the stuff in Jarvis's 1998 *Mission Impossible* diary is harmless and some of it is actually funny: there's even a joke about his mother, perhaps the best joke Jarvis had ever told. Although, apart from knowing where to find their records in Plymouth HMV I'm not sure he actually had any real idea who the Happy Mondays were.

So, 1998 then. In which Jarvis's dad wins the lottery and Jarvis decides to reinvent himself. He contemplates a name change and trying religion, plastic surgery and drugs. He buys a typewriter and writes to the BBC and he gets his hair cut at a new salon, where he appears to fall for the stylist again. Would Gabriel be sticking to the hairdresser handbook of small talk, or was I going to have teach Jarvis how to water-ski or ride a horse? At least Gabriel didn't look like Princess Diana I suppose. What am I saying? Sue didn't look like Princess Diana either. Also – and this is just for fun – I wonder if the girl giving Jarvis the scalp massage got her jumper stuck to the static electricity generated by his balloon head. Oh, and Jarvis looked nothing like Tom Cruise either by the way.

Ladies and gentlemen, 1998.

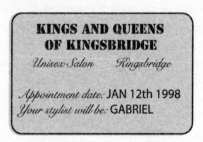

KINGS AND QUEENS OF KINGSBRIDGE

Unisex Salon   Kingsbridge

Appointment date: JAN 12th 1998
Your stylist will be: GABRIEL

JANUARY 12th 1998

I look like Tom Cruise. A young Tom Cruise (ha ha, sorry TC)
Gabriel is an angel (ha ha ha).

JANUARY 13th 1998

What Gabriel has done with my hair is a miracle. I'm not exaggerating. Maybe Gabriel is not just an angel. Maybe he is Jesus and he's come back as a hairdresser in Devon (joke) From Heaven to Devon (another joke) ((and a poem too)). Gabriel is such a better hairdresser than Sue. I don't know why I went to MARY for so long. It's so old fashioned there. It smells like boiled eggs. I'll never go back there again.

JANUARY 13th 1998

I nearly forgot. A girl gave me a head massage. It was brilliant. Very.

JANUARY 18th 1998

I was wondering if I had a whole face transplant, would I be a different person or would I just have a different face? Is there even such a thing as a face transplant?

JANUARY the twenty fourth nineteen ninety eight Possible new names
Jarvis T Switzerland
Steven
Stephen
Stefan
Maverick
Johnny One
~~Lestat DeLioncourt~~
Bryan Fantastic
~~&~~
Th omas Mapother V
~~Graham Smith~~

JANUARY 29th 1998

Dad seems really worried about Mum. So am I. She's still sick and has stayed in bed since a long time before Christmas. She is on more pills than the Happy Mondays.

FEBRUARY 2nd 1998

Last night I drew a moustache on myself with what I didn't realise at the time (obviously) was a permanent pen. I just wanted to see what I would look like with a moustache. I tried washing it off afterwards but couldn't. I scrubbed it with a toothbrush and soap but couldn't completely remove it and I woke up this morning still with a faint moustache and a red and very sore upper lip. All day people were coming in to the teahouse and asking me if I was growing a moustache. I think some people (like that fat girl) were doing it as a joke. It did get quite annoying. I was glad when the day ended. I've just been scrubbing it again and my 'moustache' has almost completely gone now, although it still feels sore and is red. I have thrown the toothbrush away (double obviously).

FEBRUARY 6th 1998

The 'moustache' has totally gone. Before my brilliant new haircut grows out I've booked a photographer to get some new pictures done. Must get some beauty sleep now (stop it cheeky). Goodnight.

FEBRUARY 7th 1998

My photo session went very well indeed. Calvin (the photographer) took hundreds of pictures. I wore make-up and kept it on for the rest of the day (I forgot). Some people were staring at me on the bus home because of the make-up. I can't wait for the photos to arrive. I think this will be the beginning of a new Jarvis Ham. Onwards and upwards Dad says. (Or is it upwards and onwards?)

FEBRUARY 20th 1998

I just saw the film *Face Off*. Wow! PS: Dad has won the lottery! £16

✝ 27.2.98.

Scientology
Buddhism
Islam ←
~~Hare Krishna~~
Judaism
~~Spiritualism~~
Rasta
Spiritualism

Bored.
Where
are my
photographs
~~Calvin?~~

MARCH 1st 1998

Really very bored. Where are my photographs Calvin?

MARCH 8th 1998

Still no pictures. My hair is growing fast. I won't recognise the person in the pictures when they finally arrive (joke).

MARCH 13th 1998

At last! My pictures arrived. Dad says they're a bit blurry and some of them are out of focus but he's not a photographic expert. The best thing though is that Calvin says he's had an offer from an agency that are really interested in taking me on as a client! They think there is a big chance they can get me a part in a television show and definitely some modelling work, which I don't mind doing. Dad says I should be careful before I give Calvin any more money. He can be so negative. More like backwards and downwards Dad. (Or downwards and backwards)

MARCH 25th 1998

A pigeon flew into the teahouse today. I hate pigeons. Dad had to leave Mum alone in bed and come in and catch it. He chased it around for a bit and then he threw a tea towel over the pigeon and picked it up and carried it outside where he released it and it flew away. It was like a magic trick. All the customers clapped. I didn't actually see any of this because I was hiding behind the counter because I hate pigeons but I guessed from the sounds I heard that that is what happened.

3.4.98.

Marryruana (spelling?)

Cocaine

E 😊

Heran

L.S.D.

Speed

Mushrooms or Harsh Cakes

glue

MAY 12th 1998

The same pigeon (don't ask me how I know it was the same one, I'm not an expert but it was the same one) was back today. He or she was outside on the pavement pecking at a chicken bone. Cannibalism comes to the South Hams. It made me feel sick and I nearly puked.

Jarvis Ham
C/o Ham and Hams Teahouse
Fore Street
Mini Addledford
Devon

BBC
Broadcasting House
London
Re: Diana

3rd July 1998

Dear the BBC

As the first anniversary of the greatest
tragedy of our modern times approaches I
have something that I think may be of
interest to you.

Last year I opened my own book of
condolence at the tearooms owned by my
parents. We have collected over two hundred
messages. I understand this doesn't sound
like an awful lot when compared to the
official book (which I have signed) but when
I tell you that the population of our
village is 937 you will see that it is
actually quite an impressive number. About
22% of the entire village!

I think that it would make for a very
interesting piece on the BBC if I were to
bring the book in and talk about it. (I have

enclosed a photograph of myself holding the book.)

Don't hesitate to get in touch if you have any questions.

I look forward to hearing from you.

Yours faithfully
Jarvis D Ham

PS: Programmes I think this would work well on: *BBC Breakfast News*, *Newsnight*, the end of the News.

JULY 23rd 1998

Calvin was on the television last night. It was one of those consumer rights shows. He was being investigated for his photography and agency scam. One of the show's presenters went to Calvin's house and asked him lots of questions that he refused to answer. And then Calvin pushed the cameraman over. I have been told that it is very unlikely that I will ever get my £480 back.

Candlelit vigil and 2 minutes silence for

DIANA

Monday August 31
At the Ham and Hams Teahouse
Fore Street
Mini Addledford

2 Minute silence
12 Noon

Candlelit vigil
Midnight

After the candlelit vigil and two-week period of mourning that followed, Jarvis asked me if I'd go swimming with him again. He wasn't expecting me to give him any lessons this time. There was no Sue to impress. He said he thought that it might be his weight that was preventing him from getting any of the acting parts he went for. He thought it may have also been the reason Calvin's agency hadn't found him any acting work: in spite of the TV show with all the wannabe models and actors claiming they were ripped off by Calvin and in spite of Calvin pushing the cameraman over and fleeing the country, Jarvis still believed it was somehow his own fault for being lazy and overweight. He'd started a diet and he wanted to get some exercise.

'But I want to go to a different pool,' he said. 'Just in case. It would be awkward if Sue *was* there.'

Basically he wanted a lift.

I'd bought a car. It was a Ford Fiesta that used to be white but had been painted red. Not spray-painted, hand painted; with a brush and a few tins of cheap emulsion. It was the mattest car in Devon. There were a million miles on the clock and the seats smelled like a wet Alsatian. It wouldn't pass its next MOT. It wouldn't even last long enough to get Jarvis and my name printed on a sticker across the top of the front windscreen.

I pulled the car up outside the Ham and Hams and I opened the front passenger door for Jarvis, who tipped the seat forward, climbed into the back and for the very first time of many, he cabbed me.

Jarvis sat in the back singing along with the radio and I drove him to the same leisure centre that Princess Diana had opened. The library was gone but there was now a PC World, a Boots and a Pizza Hut and the flumes and the wave machine that Diana had set in motion had been replaced by a six-lane swimming arena and a shallow learner pool.

There were a few other differences to my earlier experiences of swimming with Jarvis. The endless preparation before Jarvis left the changing room was still there and he still didn't have a coin – now 50p – for the locker. But now Jarvis insisted on finding a locker with a number that he liked – walking up and down the aisles carrying his clothes until he found a suitable one. It hardly mattered because he would never be able to find the locker again once he was out of the pool anyway, as without his glasses he was as blind if not slightly blinder than a bat.

When Jarvis was hunting for a lucky locker number I noticed bruises up his arms and scratches on his legs. On his right thigh there was a scab that reminded me of when we used to make fake scars and scabs when we were kids. We used to stick Sellotape onto the backs of our hands and then lick the Sellotape till it was soaking wet with spit, then we'd peel the shiny top layer off to leave just the glue and then we'd roll the glue back and forth into the shape of a scar and we'd colour it in with red felt tip pens. It was pretty realistic. Jarvis had a wound like that on his thigh. I don't think it was wet Sellotape and felt tip pen. I didn't question him about any of his injuries. I think I was afraid of what the answer might be.

Once Jarvis had finally found a locker and I'd given him the money to get the key out of the door, Jarvis plugged his ears and pegged his nose, put his goggles on and flip-flopped to the pool.

As he passed the shallow learner pool at the side of the changing rooms Jarvis appeared to stare for a long time at the mothers and water babies session going on. Some of the mothers noticed him looking and didn't like it. They shielded their babies from his apparent longing gaze. One of the mothers stepped out of the pool and walked over to us carrying her now screaming child. I could see there was about to be a misunderstanding. It had happened before in other situations. Usually near schools, or walking past a play area in a park.

It was unfortunate.

It's just, how can I put this?

You know how some men look like paedophiles?

If Jarvis had put himself up for some of those roles he would have been a lot more successful.

I tried to explain to the irate mother that Jarvis wasn't looking at the women or their children at all and he was just very short sighted without his glasses. He could have been looking at a pond full of geese for all he knew, which didn't help as it turned out the woman was pretty unreasonable or dense and demanded to know whom it was I was calling geese. And then a lifeguard came over and we were asked to leave, even though we'd done nothing wrong. Jarvis wanted to stay out of principle and as a demonstration of his innocence, and then he accused the lifeguard of being blindest even though clearly it was Jarvis who was the blindest – I had to resist with all my might to not crack that joke. Eventually I convinced Jarvis to leave by taking him to one side to reason with him, comparing pissing off the lifeguards at a swimming pool to pissing off the waiters in a restaurant.

'They're going to watch you drown Jarvis.'

He whinged for a bit and then reluctantly agreed to leave, still managing to take a ridiculous amount of time getting dressed, even though he hadn't even got wet. He still had a shower and washed and blow-dried his hair and filled the place with a sandalwood miasma.

When we finally left the pool and walked out into the leisure centre's reception area the staff behind the reception desk stared at us like we were a disgraced glam rock star and his pimp manager.

'Let's go,' I said. 'Word appears to be spreading.'

'We need to get our money back,' Jarvis said.

'What?'

Jarvis had stopped in the middle of the leisure centre reception.

'We didn't swim. We need to get our money back.'

'It doesn't matter, let's just g … What do you mean *our* money?'

'We didn't swim, we shouldn't have to pay.'

'Yes I get that. But I paid for both of us. If anything we'd be getting *my* money back.'

A small but powerful crowd was gathering in reception, watching us argue when we really should have been leaving. Gym instructors and weightlifting trainers whispered about us to karate black belts and judo coaches. Men in cap sleeved t-shirts flexed their guns, stretching their tattoos.

'*Come on*. Let's just go, we're not popular,' I said.

'It's the principle,' Jarvis said. 'We can't just leave. You get the money back and then I'll pay you back after. I need to get to a cashpoint.'

What appeared to be a ladies football team had doubled the size of the crowd in reception. We were about to become the equipment in a new Olympic sport.

'Oh for fuck's sake,' I said.

I walked over to the reception desk, eeny meeny miny moeing between which of the two sour-faced women sat behind the desk to approach for my refund – not because you're dirty, not because you're clean …

'Hello,' I smiled. 'I wonder if you can help me.' I went for the one on the left, the larger of the two sour-faced women: big women are always bubbly and great fun. I smiled again. 'We came in earlier and paid for a swim but we didn't actually swim,' I said. The sour-faced receptionist stared blankly up at me. Not so bubbly after all. I should have ipper-dipped instead. I smiled for a third time. 'We were wondering if we could have a refund.'

'His hair is wet,' she said.

I looked round at Jarvis. He had his back to me. His hair was still clearly damp.

'He had a shower.' I said.

'I thought you said you didn't go in the pool.'

'We didn't. He had a shower.'

'Why did he have a shower if you didn't go in the pool?'

I looked round at Jarvis again, hoping I might find a clever answer to that question but he still had his back to me. Although I couldn't see his face I sensed he was stuck in some kind of trance. I looked over in the direction he was facing and I saw Jennifer Fer, her hair, too, still damp from showering.

That was where the similarities between her and Jarvis ended.

Jennifer's hair was tied in a ponytail. It swung from side to side behind her as she walked in slow motion through the reception area like a shampoo ad. I heard saxophones.

Jarvis was seeing a quite different picture. He saw the woman who'd left him without even saying goodbye. The woman who'd left him all alone with nothing but a cheap plastic name badge that didn't even have her full name on. When Jarvis saw Jennifer Fer he saw someone with a heart as cold as a plunge pool – moving in normal motion, no saxophones.

Although we saw different things we were both now in a trance. We were both staring at a woman. Eliminating any doubts the leisure centre staff had that we were indeed both perverts. An angry mother with a baby would be over in a minute to ask us what it was we were staring at and then I'd call her a goose and the lifeguard would come over and throw us out again before we'd had time to leave after the first time he'd thrown us out. And then I'd have to try to get our money back from an angry fat woman and we'd be stuck in a ridiculous loop for ever.

I watched the automatic glass exit doors part for Jennifer Fer and a thousand snowy white doves flew into the air as she stepped outside.

Jarvis just saw her leave.

And he followed her.

'Have you got your tickets?'

'Sorry?'

I turned back to the sour-faced receptionist and the spell was broken. Ten hundred doves crashed to their deaths.

I went through my pockets and found the tickets. I gave them to the woman.

'Thank you,' I said.

I looked back over at the closed exit doors and wondered what was going on on the other side of them. I wondered what Jarvis was saying to Jennifer Fer. I thought of what reasons she might be coming up with for walking out on him, and most of all I wondered what she had ever seen in Jarvis Ham.

'Two adult swims,' the receptionist said and gave me back my money in the smallest denomination of coins she could find in her till. 'I'm sorry, we haven't got anything larger.' And I wanted to say, how about you? And suggest that maybe she should get off her fat arse once in a while and pop next door and try out some of the exercise equipment and facilities the building had to offer. I bet she got a staff discount and everything.

Instead I just put the money in my pocket, thanked her and gave her my best 'if it's not one thing it's another' smile – which she didn't return – and I left the building.

Jarvis and Jennifer were on the edge of the car park. Jarvis was quite animated and was saying something to Jennifer who appeared to still be getting over her surprise at suddenly seeing Jarvis again. There was something more than just surprise to her expression though. It was a look I'd seen before.

We were about thirteen years old and there was a kid at school called Michael Apricot, he was the school bully. One day Michael Apricot brought a boxing glove into school. At lunchtime he'd put the glove on and was walking around the playground punching every boy in the testicles in alphabetical order. Steven Grads was doubled over in pain and tears under the basketball net with his hands cupped between his legs, and Michael Apricot was on his way over from there to where me and Jarvis were standing. Michael Apricot had reached the letter H. Jarvis and me were next.

As he strolled over, Michael Apricot slowly punched his left palm with his gloved right fist and then he broke into a run and took a wide swing at me. I swerved and ducked to avoid Michael Apricot's gloved fist, and in doing so, instead of punching me in the balls Michael Apricot caught Jarvis on the side of the head and knocked his glasses off. They hit the hard playground and one of the lenses fell out.

Next thing Michael Apricot is on the floor next to Jarvis's broken glasses and Jarvis is sitting on top of Michael Apricot's chest shouting, 'You broke my glasses, *you broke my glasses!*' over and over as he punched Michael Apricot repeatedly in the face.

The look on Michael Apricot's face just before it started to bleed – similar to the one on my evil step dad Kenneth's face when Jarvis pulled the cake slice out of his jacket – that was the same as the look I saw on Jennifer Fer's face in the car park outside the leisure centre. It started out as a look of surprise, but then it mutated into something more.

Fear.

Jennifer Fer was terrified of Jarvis. Thank God she hadn't broken his glasses.

When she saw me walking over she relaxed slightly, she seemed pleased to see – not necessarily me – but a witness at least.

'You shouldn't say anything about her.' Were the first words I heard of what Jarvis was saying to Jennifer Fer.

'I know, I was just … I was very sorry,' she said.

'You shouldn't say anything.'

'I know, I …'

'They're all a waste of money,' Jarvis said. 'Remember? You shouldn't be sorry. You aren't sorry. Why are you saying you're sorry?'

Jennifer looked to me for help.

'Hello,' I said.

'Why did you say you were sorry?' Jarvis said, ignoring my arrival. A year of awkward silence followed while Jarvis waited for Jennifer Fer to answer him. And then Jarvis said, 'Keys.' While still staring like a maniac at Jennifer Fer.

'Keys,' he said again.

Jarvis held his open palm out to me.

I realised he was talking to me.

'What?' I said.

'Keys.'

I took my car keys out of my pocket and put them in his hand.

'Bye,' he said, not really to either of us and he turned and walked away through the car park.

I stood with Jennifer Fer and we watched Jarvis walking purposefully in the general direction of where I'd parked the car. I knew he'd never find it without me. He wasn't very observant. He'd have no idea of the car's make or colour. He could end up trying the keys in the door of a horsebox or a yellow submarine without really knowing for sure it was the wrong vehicle. He tripped on a stone or something and nearly fell over, but it wasn't funny. Although I wish somebody had been filming it because I knew it would be funny later. He disappeared behind a line of cars.

'I should get back to work,' Jennifer said.

'Sorry about that,' I said to her. She was definitely prettier than I remembered. I heard saxophones again and another six years of a different kind of awkward silence passed. A tumbleweed drifted by and then we did that thing that happens in films to illustrate sexual tension, where two people speak at once: I said, 'You know …' And Jennifer said, 'Look …'

We both laughed, although her laugh was more of a loud breath.

'You know, we came and looked for you,' I said.

'Really?'

Seriously, I definitely hadn't remembered her being this beautiful.

'All over Totnes. Up to the castle and everything.'

Jennifer Fer was about to say something and then decided against it. I think she was reminiscing. Thinking about her short time as Jarvis's girlfriend. Trying to work out why she left him without telling him she was leaving him. Some acceptable, reasonable explanation she could give to me for her being the bad guy. Jennifer Fer turned it all over in her head. She made two columns: negatives and positives, she totted it all up, did the maths and then ended up back at the thing she was going to say in the first place.

'He's a bit strange.'

She lifted her arm to push her fringe out of her eyes (green).

'They should put it on his gravestone,' I said.

Under her sports anorak Jennifer Fer was wearing a red polo shirt.

There was a name badge pinned to it that said PIZZA HUT – JENNIFER CHARLETON, TEAM MEMBER.

'You changed your name,' I said.

She looked down at the badge.

'I got married,' she said.

'Oh.'

'It's traditional.'

The drive home was going to be horrible. I wondered which Jarvis would be waiting for me when I went back to the car. Sulky Jarvis: staring silently out the window all the way back. Inquisitive Jarvis: *What did she say about me? Why did she leave? Why were you talking to her for so long? Do you love Jennifer Fer?* Or Jarvis in denial: pretending it had never happened as he sang along with chart hits and tried to instigate car games all the way home?

'I should get back,' Jennifer said, nodding towards the Pizza Hut on the other side of the car park. I realised I was still looking at her name badge. I didn't want her to think I was a sex pervert. Especially after what had just happened in the pool.

As I was walking back to the car I found Jarvis trying to force the key into a blue Toyota Picnic people carrier with a white poodle dog in the back. I pointed to where my car was, he gave me the keys,

I opened the front passenger door and Jarvis tipped the seat forward and climbed into the back. He never said a word about Jennifer all the way back home. Not a word.

DEAN BANTHAM AND SHANE PRIOR

There were a lot of dead animals on the A303 today. Foxes and badgers, squirrels and a deer, those were the ones I could recognise as we drove past their corpses at the side of the road. The windscreen too was spattered with death. Brown, red and yellow autumnal coloured blood and guts of what I presume were dead flies or mosquitoes or some other A road kamikaze insect.

All this road kill naturally made me think about Road Fill. I thought of Dean Bantham, stepping out into the corridor outside the toilet, drying his hands on his trousers – because I doubt the hand dryer was working. He was in a good mood, he remembered that, he'd had a successful day at work and had stopped at the Mister Breakfast to buy a bottle of wine to drink with his dinner when he got home. Why did a roadside restaurant whose customers were mostly motorists sell alcohol? Dean often wondered. He'd talked about it when he was being interviewed about the attack for a trashy tabloid magazine called *My Strange but True Life*. He said 'It's a bit like having a cocktail bar in the scrub up room in a hospital operating theatre.' Dean Bantham had obviously been working on his memorable interview quotes.

Dean hadn't come far before stopping at the Mister Breakfast to buy booze. He worked just seven miles away, taking photographs at, and for, Exeter International Airport. His days were usually spent hanging around in the Arrivals lounge waiting for members of barely famous boy and girl bands and trying to recognise people off the TV that he'd been tipped off would be coming through customs. He often had to carry a picture of the famous person he was waiting to photograph and keep referring to it so that he'd recognise them when they arrived. Dean rarely took photographs of anyone he'd actually seen on the television or had even heard sing on the radio. Dean never listened to the radio.

That day had been different though. Dean Bantham was about to finish work after a long and slow day taking pictures of the CEO of one of the airport's minor airlines (three small planes, two pilots) to go on the wall of the VIP lounge. He'd packed up his cameras and re-telescoped his tripod and was about to leave the airport when somebody he actually recognised walked through the nothing to declare corridor and into the Arrivals lounge. Dean Bantham had always admired the films of this actress. He'd told the magazine he would have gone as far as to say she was his favourite actress of all time.

'The way she walked through the airport. Such grace. Humility. You know. Some of the soap stars and the reality show people I have to take pictures of, you know, they *want* to be seen. With their big sunglasses, you know, indoors in the daytime, so they make sure they get noticed and then they're all rude to us for taking a picture. When we've been asked to be there by their own PR company in the first place. She was different though. Classy. Just strolled through Arrivals, no entourage, carrying her own bags. And I asked her if she'd mind stopping for a photo; no problem at all she said. She posed and smiled. Lovely. Proper.'

After that Dean Bantham had started driving home. He was feeling good and thought he'd like a drink with his dinner. He was going to put on his favourite film starring the actress he'd just photographed. It was Saturday night and there'd be nothing on TV anyway. Just talent shows and probably a soap about a hospital. Dean Bantham hated talent shows and soap operas.

Stopping off at the Mister Breakfast involved driving in a circle and coming back the way he'd just driven but it was still the nearest place Dean knew that was open where he could buy a bottle of wine on his way home.

Dean Bantham had walked into the restaurant and based on his philosophy that you should 'never walk past a toilet when you're on a car journey' he went straight through to the toilets before getting his wine. There were no other customers in the restaurant and nobody had noticed him come in.

'The next thing I knew, *bang*. Out like a light. I haven't been able to work since. I can't focus. That's not a photographer joke by the way.'

Dean Bantham was thirty-six years old when he was attacked in the first Breakfast Killer incident. A white male between twenty-five and forty, driving home and stopping for something to eat or drink and to use the toilet. The victim of the second attack, the one in the car park out the back of what was now a diner, he was thirty-one, a single white male on his way home after a long shift as a porter in the Kidney unit of Royal Devon and Exeter Hospital. Shane Prior lived alone and couldn't cook. He would often make bold self-deprecating claims about how he'd never boiled an egg and didn't know how you cooked toast. He was probably overqualified to get a job at Mister Breakfast. So instead he became one of their most regular customers. Every other day or so Shane would stop in on his way home from work for a Mister Breakfast dinner. Depending on what day of the week it was he would always choose the same thing from the menu. It was a Monday evening. Monday was scampi and chips, with peas and a slice of lemon. He didn't have too far to drive so he ordered a small lager as well.

On the way back to his car he was hit over the back of the head. He said he saw nothing; the attack came completely out of the blue. He thought he'd heard a car door shutting shortly before but didn't remember seeing any other cars. He said he felt like he'd been ambushed, which prompted the press and the police to add the word SOLDIER? to their list of possible suspects.

When the police said on TV that Shane Prior had nothing particular in common with Dean Bantham and when they said much the same thing again with each subsequent attack my girlfriend must have been out or watching a DVD.

Something else my girlfriend had said to me last night during our argument about Jarvis was how she didn't feel good about me driving back from London at night on my own. She said I fitted the demographic of the Breakfast Killer's victims.

'I'll be fine,' I said. 'And anyhow, I won't be on my own. I'll have Jarvis with me.' Which I knew wasn't true and only seemed to make her worry even more anyway.

'Well don't stop at least.'

'What if I'm hungry?'

'Take a packed lunch.'

'I might need to use the toilet.'

'I'm serious,' she said. She didn't like me teasing her. I hugged her and told her I'd be fine and made a little joke about how I'd be too old for the killer's tastes soon anyway. She gave me a loving jab in the ribs and made me promise that I'd be careful. 'It's not safe out there for you,' she said.

She made me feel like a Whitechapel prostitute in the 1800s.

JARVIS GIVES SOMETHING BACK

1999

Give blood
 Work in a charity shop
Sponsored run (is there such a thing as a
 quarter marathon? (find out))
Per form in old peoples home
Sponsored swim
Perform in mental hospital
Take leftover scones and cakes to homeless
people
Charity single
Clear people's paths of snow (if it snows)
Shav~~e all hair~~off for charity
Dye hair for charity
G row a beard for charity
Sit in ba~~th of bak~~ked beans (disgusting) for
charity
Parachute jump
sponsored walk
~~Dressing up day~~ at the Ham and Hams
Quiz at the Ha m and Hams
Face painting

At the end of 1998 Jarvis appeared in a local amateur dramatic production of the pantomime *Cinderella*. I went along to watch. In many ways I wished I hadn't. Many ways. The whole show struck me as a poorly disguised (many ways) excuse for some of the older male members of the cast to dress in women's clothing, put on too much make-up and talk in Pythonesque high-pitched voices. It was actually quite creepy. There were kids in the show. I wanted to call the police. It all seemed to go on for about fourteen hours and then just as I and most of the audience were losing the will to live it finally stopped.

For an interval.

A cup of weak tea and a plain biscuit later and it all started again. I started to think that it would never end and I wouldn't ever be allowed to leave and I'd eventually die in that church hall. I would never get to write the witty 'They don't call Him God for nothing' slogan that would never appear on a sign outside. Nobody would see the sign and as a result they'd think, *this church is so boring, let's go somewhere else.* But the nearest alternative place of worship wouldn't have one of my signs outside either and the people would give up on going to church altogether and go home and watch porn instead. Leaky roofs would not be repaired and the church organs would remain out of tune, driving yet more people away.

Eventually both churches would be sold to a furniture warehouse chain or become lap dancing clubs. People would soon stop reading the Bible and singing Christmas carols. They'd seek out alternatives and turn to alcohol and drugs and to religious cults and the dark side. A lot of goats and virgins were going to die for this awful am dram production of *Cinderella*.

Jarvis played the character of Buttons. His mum had made him a costume. She must have had her sewing machine set up on a table by her bed because she was ill at the time: too ill to make it to the performance – every cloud. Jarvis's mum had made Jarvis a blue satin suit. She'd sewn gold ribbon piping into the trousers and jacket. She added frills to one of her husband's white shirts and made a blue satin hat with more gold ribbon around the top and the brim. Mrs Ham's costumier skills had come a long way since her King Tut cocktail dress and tea towel outfit and Jarvis actually looked pretty good.

Also, I know the competition was only a bunch of unconvincing transvestites and a few primary school children, but nevertheless, Jarvis was the best thing in the show. I was actually quite proud of him.

When the pantomime had finally finished and the audience were released, I waited for Jarvis outside the church to give him a lift home. On the short drive back to his house he told me he how the proceeds from *Cinderella* were going to a local hospice and once the takings from the half time tea and biscuits were included they expected to make almost £35. Jarvis said he wanted to spend the next year of his life giving something back. I would like to think that I made a joke about how he hadn't really taken anything away yet.

Jarvis didn't keep much of a record of his heroic period of altruism but I was there with him a lot of the time and I did.

MONDAY JANUARY 18th 1999

MARTIN LUTHER KING JR BIRTHDAY OBSERVANCE, HOLIDAY USA
I had a phone call this afternoon from a distraught Jarvis
asking me to drive to Plymouth and pick him up. He's been
collecting money for a cancer charity since last Wednesday
and this morning some kids had come up to him outside
British Home Stores and tried to post coins into the top of
his head saying they thought he was one of those blind boy
collection boxes. They ignored his cries of protest and kept
banging the top of his head with coins. While Jarvis was
distracted one of the kids had snatched his collection bucket
and they'd all run off. When I got there Jarvis was
hyperventilating outside BHS. Somebody from the store had
given him a paper bag to breathe into. When he calmed
down Jarvis said he'd told the whole story to the charity but
they didn't believe him and he would have to pay the money
back. He'd forgotten to bring any money or his cash card
with him and we had to go to my bank and draw out the
stolen money. We took it straight to the charity's offices and
it was only on the drive home afterwards that I realised we
could have lied about the amount of money we thought
Jarvis had collected.

SATURDAY FEBRUARY 6th 1999

The blood transfusion lorry came to the village today and
Jarvis and me went along and gave blood. I say gave blood.
What actually happened – you couldn't make it up. Jarvis
kept snatching his hand away when the nurse was trying to
take a tiny drop of sample blood from his fingertip and on
the final attempt to get the needle into his finger Jarvis

pulled his hand away so sharply that he knocked a load of
stuff off a trolley and a different nurse walking by at the time
slipped on something and fell flat on her back. An
ambulance was called to take the nurse to hospital for a
possible spinal injury and Jarvis felt faint and had to lie
down, even though he hadn't donated any of his blood.
When he asked if he could still have a cup of tea and a
biscuit, the nurse who'd been attempting to take Jarvis's
blood sample told him to just fuck off. We pretty much had
to do a runner down the lorry steps.

On Valentine's Day Jarvis released a charity single. There were loads
of massive stars singing on it and Phil Collins played the drums. I
found the one and only copy of *Giving Back* in the big leather
actor's suitcase. Like with Jarvis's debut solo album I didn't need to
listen to it because the CD inside the sleeve was a copy of 'Barbie
Girl' by Aqua and I'd already heard it.

He's still signed to EMI.

JARVIS HAM
GIVING BACK

**Featuring Elton John, Robbie Williams, Kylie Minogue,
Céline Dion, Ronan Keating, Spice Girls, Madonna,
Bono, Tom Cruise, George Michael, Steps, The Corrs,
Janet Jackson, Cher, Simply Red, B*Witched and LeAnn
Rimes with Phil Collins on drums**

All the proceeds from the sales of this
single go to the Jarvis Ham Foundation

FRIDAY MARCH 5th 1999

Last night I picked up Jarvis and two boxes of Ham and Hams cakes and drove him and them to Plymouth to look for hungry and homeless people. Like with the blood fiasco last month you couldn't make it up. To be honest I think some of the people sleeping on the streets that we approached weren't as happy as Jarvis had hoped or expected they'd be when we offered them fairy cakes and fondant fancies. I think they thought we were taking the piss. We then somehow managed to get into an argument with the Salvation Army who were dishing out soup. It was the most ridiculous turf war of all time. Jarvis was wearing his *Top Gun* replica navy pilot's jacket, complete with fake fur collar and covered in *Top Gun* replica patches, that he'd paid a lot of money to an American fancy dress mail order company for. His hair was thick with gel and his fringe was shaped into a point so stiff and sharp you could keep your receipts on it. Facing Jarvis on the opposing side of the turf war battlefield there were six fully uniformed members of the Sally Army with a large saucepan of minestrone soup and a carrier bag of bread rolls. There was a lot of finger pointing and name calling and then a load of drunk women on a hen night turned up and started jeering and showing their tits to the homeless men. The two sides reached an impasse and the Salvation Army marched off in a sulk and we walked back to the car with Jarvis's undistributed cakes. The homeless didn't get any less hungry by the whole stupid display but they did at least have a bit of free entertainment on a cold March night.

On the day after his twenty-seventh birthday Jarvis answered an advert in the paper and sent a cheque for £25 to the Big Hearts for Hurt Hearts charity. In return he'd have permission to use the charity's name and collect donations on their behalf as an official 'Big Hearts for Hurt Hearts Friend'. A week later Jarvis received his collector's pack of stickers, fund raising tips and a laminate with the name of the charity on. The accompanying letter told Jarvis there were three levels of Big Hearts for Hurt Hearts Friends: bronze, silver and gold. If he raised enough money to be a gold collector Jarvis would receive a certificate with his name on and would be put forward for press, radio and TV appearances on behalf of the charity and would be photographed holding a giant cheque with the soap star who was the charity's patron.

Jarvis was going to be a Gold Hearted Friend. No doubt about that.

He started with a tabletop sale outside the Ham and Hams Teahouse. His dad wasn't too happy with it. He thought Jarvis's table, topped with old toys, books and videos made the pavement outside the Teahouse look untidy. The table also blocked access to that part of Fore Street – forcing people to either step into the road or cross over to the other side. This also upset Mary in the hair-dressers next door and the apple-faced young men in the estate agents. It was all resolved before lunchtime when Jarvis gave up anyway, after a long morning of no things sold and three things stolen.

The following weekend Jarvis convinced his dad they should both wear fancy dress for a day at the Ham and Hams and get customers to donate money. Jarvis smoothed the creases out of his Buttons costume and his dad hung some fake gold chains around his neck and blacked up as Mr T for the day. Mr *Tea*. It was supposed to be a joke, but it didn't really work because Jarvis's dad spent most of the day explaining to old ladies who he was supposed to be and then explaining who Mr T was, who the A-Team were and so on.

The casual racism didn't seem to bother anyone at all.

As a Big Hearts for Hurt Hearts Friend Jarvis also did a sponsored walk around the village, hosted a quiz in the Ham and Hams, dyed his hair in the colours of whatever flag his dad unfurled on Wednesday – which turned out to be the red, blue and orange of Armenia – and donated half his wages and all his tips to the charity. By the end of his third week of fundraising, which had also included car washing, face painting, dog walking, a massively unsuccessful sponsored silence and shaving the results of three weeks of sponsored beard growth into a series of comedy moustaches – all the way from Fu Manchu to Hitler, via handlebar, Mark Spitz and pencil – Jarvis had collected £487.34, more than enough for his Gold Hearted Friend certificate and his moment in the limelight with the soap star.

He put all the money he'd raised into his bank and wrote a cheque for £487.34, posted it to the Big Hearts for Hurt Hearts PO box and waited for his certificate and his photo op with the soap star and the big cheque.

You don't need to be Hercule Poirot or have psychic powers to have worked out – probably round about the moment Jarvis wrote that first cheque for £25 – what happens next.

For a long time it was nothing.

Just a lot of waiting for the postman. And then on the afternoon of May 24th Jarvis was in the Ham and Hams slicing a strawberry covered New York cheesecake when the bell above the door tinkled and two policemen came in. And in front of a busy-for-a-Monday-afternoon teahouse Jarvis was read his rights and taken away for questioning about his part in a massive £250,000 charity fraud.

Two days later he was back at home watching television, completely cleared of any crime other than being a gullible patsy. The programme Jarvis was watching on TV was the same consumer rights show that Calvin the bogus photographer and talent agent had appeared on less than a year earlier. Calvin – whose name was now Kelvin – was back on the show again, refusing to answer questions from the show's presenter, before there was a scuffle and he pushed the cameraman over. And then the programme cut back to the television studio to another presenter sitting on the edge of a table, reading a statement from the soap star named as the Big Hearts for Hurt Hearts patron, declaring that he had no knowledge of, or connection with, the fake charity whatsoever. The presenter then went on to say it was unlikely that anyone duped by Calvin/Kelvin would get their money back.

It didn't snow for long enough for Jarvis to clear any paths, he was running out of pools to do any sponsored swimming in, the charity shops were all fully staffed at the moment thank you and there wasn't such a thing as a quarter marathon in the Devon area (although I don't think Jarvis really tried finding out, the same goes for parachute jumping). Jarvis did perform in a mental hospital. It was with the *Cinderella* am dram group again, in a stage version of the TV show *Lovejoy*. The older male members of the cast weren't dressed as women this time and there were no children in the show to make Jarvis look good, and his portrayal of Lovejoy's assistant and dogsbody Eric Catchpole was bad enough for word to reach the old people's home, who cancelled their upcoming *Lovejoy* booking a fortnight later.

```
                                    Devon Dram
                        Amateur Dramatic Society
                               June 21st 1999
```

```
Dearest Jarvis,
It is with greatest regret that I write this
letter but after much consideration and
discussion with the other members I'm afraid
that perhaps we aren't the right am dram
group for you.
   We wish you the greatest success with your
future.

Yours sincerely,
Geoffrey Gracemount
```

Jarvis Ham
C/o Ham and Hams Teahouse
Fore Street
Mini Addledford
Devon

BBC
Broadcasting House
London

Re: Diana

10th August 1999

Dear BBC

I was disappointed that you passed on this
opportunity last year but I suggest again
that as the second anniversary of what still
is the greatest tragedy of our modern times
approaches I have something that I think may
be of interest to you.

The year before last I opened my own book
of condolence at the tearooms owned by my
parents. We have collected over two hundred
messages. The population of our village is
only 948 (937 when the book was closed) so
you will see that it is actually quite an
impressive number. Which was almost 22% of
the village.

I still believe that it would make an
interesting piece on the BBC if I were to
bring the book in and talk about it.

```
   Again, don't hesitate to get in touch if
you have any questions.
   I look forward to hearing from you.


Yours faithfully
Jarvis D Ham
```

It was starting to rain again. I put on the windscreen wipers and turned up the car radio. It was a good song for driving in the rain. The rhythm of the wipers was soon in perfect synchronicity with the beat of the song. The rain and the wipers also cleared some of the death from the windscreen. I checked the road behind and it was clear and the road ahead was clear too, not a blind bend in sight. I changed gear and increased the weight of my foot on the accelerator.

'What are you doing?' Jarvis said, feeling the surge of speed beneath him and looking up from painting his nails: yes, painting his nails.

'There's a rainbow,' I said.

'So?'

'I want to see if I can drive under it.'

'Why?'

'I just wondered if it's possible.'

'Of course it isn't possible.'

'How do you know?'

The rainbow was an almost perfect semicircle, like a child's drawing of a rainbow. I dipped my head and tried to get a fuller view of it. The left side of the rainbow partially disappeared for a bit as the road turned and then it was there again: a perfect arc. I changed gear again. The old gearbox would have crunched and screamed in protest but this new one didn't make a sound.

Jarvis screwed the lid back onto his jar of nail varnish and reached for his seatbelt.

'I feel sick,' he said. He pulled the seatbelt across his chest but still didn't fasten it. If I slammed on the brakes and ducked he'd go through the windscreen.

'Slow down.'

If I slammed on the brakes hard enough I might be able to launch him under the rainbow. Was that possible I wondered?

'I feel sick.'

Like a human cannonball.

'I feel really sick.'

I pictured Jarvis being loaded into a giant cannon.

'Open a window,' I said.

'It's too windy.' Jarvis gently touched his hair like he was making sure it was all still there.

A brass band was playing. The crowd were slow-handclapping, a clown was holding a giant matchstick, about to light the fuse. Just slam on the brakes, duck and it will all be over.

'*Slow down.*'

The rainbow seemed to be even more distant now. The closer we got to it the further it seemed to get away from us. We were coming up to a roundabout and I eased off the accelerator. Jarvis relaxed. He started to open his nail varnish again. But hey, this was my car game. I would be the one who would say when it was over.

'Shall we pick up a hitcher Jarvis?'

'What?' He stopped unscrewing the lid.

Just before the roundabout there was a man wearing a hooded raincoat, he was carrying something, probably a sign with the word LONDON written on it.

'No,' Jarvis said. 'Categorically, no.'

'Come on, it might be someone interesting.'

'He looks dirty.'

'It might be someone famous.'

'*Hitchhiking?*'

'His limo might have broken down.'

'He looks like he smells.'

'Let's just see where he wants to go.'

'*No.*'

It was like poking a wasps nest with a stick or throwing pebbles at a crocodile. I looked at Jarvis in the mirror, huffing and puffing like a hamster eating a balloon, or vice versa, and I wondered how far I could push him before I got to see for myself whatever it was that Jennifer Fer, Kenneth and Michael Apricot had seen. What I really needed was a boxing glove or some mistletoe and a job in a food hall.

I drove onto the roundabout, passing the hitcher who was holding a piece of cardboard that did indeed say LONDON, although he'd misjudged the amount of space to size of letter ratio and it actually said LONDO. When we came out the other side of the roundabout the rainbow would be gone. I wouldn't be able to say whether we had driven under it. Jarvis was probably right. I imagine it's impossible.

The first roundabout exit used to lead to a hotel and a Mister Breakfast. Neither of them was there any more. Shut down and demolished, cleared away in skips and the land already overgrown with weeds, grass and the kind of everyday objects men reeled in on the end of their fishing lines in silent comedies: bicycle wheels, a pram and discarded items of clothing that it was best to not dwell on how they might have ended up there. There was a strip of blue and white POLICE LINE DO NOT CROSS tape caught in the branches of a tree.

MARK HALWELL

When people watching the News with the sound turned down saw a photograph of Mark Halwell appear on the television screen they said,

'Thank God. They've got him.'

Mark Halwell's wild eyes and crazy hair made it look as though he'd had his fingers in an open plug socket when the photograph was taken. There were heavy bags beneath his wild eyes, his skin was blotchy and yet somehow bloodless, he had a broken nose and there was a small but obvious scar where the hair didn't grow on one side of his lopsided moustache. On his neck there was a tattoo of a black snake eating a swan. Mark Halwell looked more like an offender than a victim.

Mark Halwell was on his way home from the races when he went into the Mister Breakfast. Up until then it had been his lucky day. He'd just won £760 on an accumulator bet and was the happy side of drunk. He'd left his car in the racecourse car park and got a lift from a friend as far as the roadside restaurant on the roundabout by the hotel, where his wife was going to come and pick him up and drive him the rest of the way home. In the back of his friend's car he dialled his wife's number on his mobile and as he waited for her to answer he picked up his winning wad of wrinkled ten and twenty pound notes and sniffed it. The smell of old money is horrible unless you've got a lot of it.

The car pulled into the Mister Breakfast as Mark Halwell was talking to his wife on the phone. He opened the passenger door, climbed out, nodded his thanks to his friend and shut the car door.

As the car drove away Mark Halwell was telling his wife about his lucky day at the races; he told her he'd take her out for a meal at the weekend to celebrate and to make up for ringing her up when he was drunk and for making her have to drive all the way out to the Mister Breakfast in the middle of the night to get him. He told her he loved her and arranged to meet her outside in about ten or fifteen minutes' time.

'I'll just go in for a piss,' he said.

Those were the last words of Mark Halwell.

When his wife arrived the police were already there, wrapping the car park in so much plastic tape that it looked like a puppy was on the loose with a toilet roll. The police helicopter was up above Janine Halwell, its Doppler effect getting higher and lower as it circled the area shining a spotlight on the road below and the surrounding countryside all around. All they could find were cars, empty fields and a few startled cows.

There were three police vehicles on the ground and Janine Halwell heard the assorted sirens of more on the way. Once she'd worked out what was happening her own screaming would drown out all but the nearest sirens until she was taken away to sit in the back of one of the police cars, where a hot drink was brought out to her from the Mister Breakfast. A female police officer put a blanket around Janine Halwell's shoulders and removed the chocolate flake and mini marshmallows from the cup of hot chocolate while a plainclothes detective asked questions about her husband.

She was in no fit state to answer questions but it was important for the police to get as much information as possible early on. This was the start of what they called the Golden Hour, when the clues were fresh, the trail hot and the witnesses alert. They needed to seal the area off to avoid contamination and collect evidence and talk to any witnesses before they forgot what they might have seen or read in the newspapers about what it was they might have seen and started to subconsciously make stuff up.

Inside the roadside restaurant police questioned the three customers and two members of staff, none of whom had seen or heard anything. Another two officers were in the reception of the hotel next door asking the same questions of the hotel's four guests and one member of staff and getting the same blank looks and answers.

A photographer was on his way to take pictures of the scene and someone else would mark a point near Mark Halwell's head – his eyes still wild and his hair crazy but both equally dead. There were no obvious injuries. They'd have to turn him over and see the back of his head all caved in before they'd start to make educated guesses as to the cause of Mark Halwell's death. He'd been hit over the head. More times than in previous attacks. Either it took longer for Mark Halwell to die or the Breakfast Killer was starting to enjoy him or herself. More police and forensics team members would arrive, climb into white suits to measure things and dust for fingerprints and talk into Dictaphones, just like on the TV.

It was too soon to say at the time but blunt force trauma was the most likely cause of Mark Halwell's death. The murder weapon was a blunt object again – baseball bat and piece of wood added to the spanner and monkey wrench on the previous crimes' Cluedo board pieces list, and presumably carpenter and baseball player would be added to the list of possible suspect occupations.

The £760 in foul-smelling ten and twenty pound notes found in Mark Halwell's pocket told the police that once again robbery was not the motive.

* * *

The sight of Stonehenge coming up in the distance is always a welcome one on the drive to London or back. It always feels like I've reached the halfway point in the journey. Today was no different. Seeing the circle of ancient standing stones coming up ahead in the field on our left made me feel like we were getting somewhere. Not too far to go now. It'll all be over soon.

'You know how your parents lie to you?' Jarvis said.

'No. What do you mean?'

'The way they tell you things when you're young that aren't true but you believe them because you're young and because they're your parents?'

'No, still not with you.'

'My dad told me that the reason Stonehenge is the way it is. The way the stones are all arranged and everything. It's got nothing to do with ancient rituals or religions or anything, they were laid out like that for target practice by the Army in, I don't know, 1950 or something. Soldiers arranged the stones in a circle and then put the stones on top using a crane. I've only just realised that's not true.'

A small crowd of what were most likely tourists were standing behind the rope barrier around Stonehenge, taking photographs of the prehistoric stones.

'Literally, just that second. I suddenly realised my dad was lying,' Jarvis said. 'Also, he used to tell me that the South Hams was named after our family. *The whole area*. We were supposed to be some big important Devon family in the past or something. It wasn't true. He was lying again. Do you know where it comes from?'

'Where what comes from?' I said.

'The name. South Hams. It comes from the old English word hamme.' He spelled it out for me. 'H.A.M.M.E. Which means a sheltered place. I read it in a leaflet that was on the teahouse counter. Another lie. Why do our parents lie to us?'

'I don't think they're really lies as such.'

'Well they aren't true.'

'Yeah but, not lies.'

'What are they then?'

'I don't know, fibs maybe. Fairy tales.'

'Fairy tales? How?'

'Okay, not fairy tales.' God, he was annoying. 'What I mean is, they aren't malicious lies, they're fun lies.'

'*Fun* lies?'

'Okay. For example, and this is a bad example, but say if you tell your kids that Father Christmas is coming and then you spend all your hard earned money on presents that you sneak into a pillowcase in the middle of the night for them on Christmas Eve just to make your kids happy. Is that a lie?'

'Yes.' Seriously, he's really annoying.

'But compared to say, some of Hitler's whoppers or, I don't know, the moon landings or Elvis not being dead, your dad's lies aren't really so bad.'

'Is that you trying to sound clever again?' Jarvis said.

'Not intentionally.'

Jarvis looked out the window for a bit at the tourists with their cameras and guidebooks and at the druids and hippies who'd driven and flown from all over the world to join the protest to stop the bulldozers beginning their work on the construction of the Stonehenge Maccy D's next to the visitor centre.

'Did you know my dad used to be a junior swimming champion?' he said.

'No. Really?'

'No,' he said. 'Not really. It's another lie. He used to tell me how he'd been born with webbed feet and it made him a brilliant swimmer and he'd won all these medals and cups.'

I wanted to ask, 'Like Sue?' But thought it would be best not to.

'When he was a teenager,' Jarvis continued. 'He told me his swimming career ended on the day he cut through the webbed skin between his toes with a pair of nail scissors.'

'Jeeeesus,' I said.

'There are plenty more where that came from.'

Jarvis carried on telling me about all the white lies his dad had told him throughout his life, and I wanted to say 'like father like son' but I didn't. He told me about how his dad had never really met the Beatles and hadn't walked barefoot on hot coals and how Coca-Cola wasn't actually invented in Devon like his dad had always told him it was. And he said that for years he'd believed his dad when he'd told him that Mister Breakfast, the Little Chef and the Happy Eater were three real people who went to catering college together in the nineteen sixties.

My favourite lie that Jarvis's dad had told him was how his own father – Jarvis's grandfather – had a pet myna bird that he'd taught to speak with a vocabulary of over four hundred words, including some basic Latin. The myna bird also used to answer the phone. I loved that one. Jarvis didn't find it amusing. He said it was just another lie, and I wanted to say something about black pots and kettles but I hate people who say that almost as much as people who describe things as doing exactly what they say on the tin.

While Jarvis was talking about his big fat liar of a father, although it made him quite angry, at least he wasn't bored.

It wasn't just Jarvis getting bored that I wanted to avoid, it was letting him have too much time to think. I didn't want Jarvis's mind wandering back to some of the dark places it had been to lately.

A few miles back I'd looked in the rear-view mirror and seen Jarvis starting to fidget in the back seat, making a fist and drumming on his thigh. Breathing heavily. He looked like he might be feeling carsick again. But I knew it was something else. He was tapping his foot restlessly and checking his pockets for things that weren't there. I watched him in the mirror, squeezing his eyes shut tightly as if trying to either remember or more likely forget something. I knew what was wrong. I was surprised he'd made it as far as he had to be honest. If his mind was heading into one of those dark places the least I could do was give him a torch.

'There's some bits in a carrier bag back there,' I said. 'Under my seat,' I wanted to say, 'in case of emergency', but I didn't.

Jarvis ignored me for a while.

Just for show.

We both knew that.

But it was something we didn't talk about. The elephant in the room had come out of the room and had got in the car with us before I'd even started the engine. After enough just-for-show time had passed Jarvis reached under the seat, picked the supermarket carrier bag up from the floor and looked inside.

'There are some plastic cups in the bag,' I said.

Jarvis didn't touch the crisps, nuts or any of the oranges or bananas that were also in the carrier. That was okay. I'd only put them in there to make him feel better about himself. They were the lettuce and pickle in the obese man's Big Mac. The Diet Pepsi ordered with the bucket of chicken wings and curly fries. Jarvis could kid himself and me that when he chose the wine rather than the crisps or the oranges he was just making a random selection. It just happened to be the wine every time.

His name is Jarvis Ham and he's an alcoholic.

Jarvis unscrewed the bottle, poured himself a cup of wine and slowly sipped it. The results seemed both instant and miraculous.

How could such a small amount of cheap German wine do that to an alcoholic? Could it really be that powerful? Was the need for booze all in his mind? Could I have achieved the same results with half a placebo pint of flat Shlöer decanted into the wine bottle? Why wasn't I a doctor?

When Jarvis had needed to get a few things from the shop at Road Fill, he meant alcohol. When he'd stood by the shelf of tissues and Travel Scrabble at Road Fill, he was looking for alcohol. When Jarvis had gone into a shop and bought an apple, a banana, a clarinet and a diplodocus, he was buying alcohol. Everything else was trimmings. Bullshit and trimmings. The salad on a fat man's plate. Jarvis would try to pass the bottles of crap wine and cooking sherry off as an afterthought – *Oh, while I'm here I may as well get a couple of bottles*. But they never were an afterthought.

When I went to Jarvis's house I'd sometimes play a game of find the hidden booze. While Jarvis was out of the room I'd go through his kitchen cupboards and bedroom drawers. I'd find half a bottle of English sherry in the cupboard above the sink with the breakfast cereal or a can of Crucial Brew under it with the Vim and the Ajax and the mop stained with Jarvis's alcoholic sick. There were tonic wines under the bath and a bottle of Blue Nun in his dad's garden shed.

There was no joy in Jarvis's drinking. He never went to the pub. He hated pubs. He'd been picked on more in pubs for the way he looked than when he was at school. In his most local local there was a piece of graffiti on the wall of the gents that said *JARVIS HAM SUCKS COCKS*, followed by his phone number. Besides, the pubs weren't even open when Jarvis had his first drink of the day.

Jarvis was a home drinker. He'd have his first tipple shortly after and often before he got out of bed, a cheeky Chardonnay with his Weetabix or a Merlot to complement his boiled egg and toast soldiers. Sometimes Jarvis's drinking would go on for the rest of the day, sometimes it wouldn't. And he never ever seemed drunk. I guess because he always was. Seriously, why aren't I a doctor?

I remember the day Jarvis had his first drink. It was like he was playing a role in a soap opera with a message about the perils of drinking.

1. He has his first drink.
2. He is immediately drunk.
3. He shouts for a while.
4. He swears at somebody.
5. He falls over.
6. He pukes up.
7. Cries.
8. End credits

Followed by an announcement with a helpline phone number for those affected by any of the events they'd just witnessed scrolling along the foot of the TV screen.

After his first drink Jarvis didn't have another one for a very long time but the damage was done. Jarvis was hooked. An alcoholic waiting to happen.

JARVIS BURIES A MILLENNIUM TIME CAPSULE

On the last New Year's Eve of the nineteen nineties I drove Jarvis out to the Golden Parachutes Holiday and Retirement Village beneath the M5. In the boot of my recently new car – a silver Vauxhall Omega Elite – there was a garden fork and spade, a large round cake tin Jarvis had 'borrowed' from the Ham and Hams, a bottle of something called Tollinger champagne and a cardboard box containing all the things he wanted to bury to mark the end of the millennium.

I parked the car in the Golden Parachutes car park and we carried everything over to the small garden at the side of the Hams family static home, where I started digging with the fork while Jarvis watched and critiqued my digging style. Once I'd cleared the turf and broken into the hard topsoil I switched to the spade and dug a hole big enough for *The Jarvis Ham Time Capsule*, which was actually the large round cake tin he'd borrowed and would return to the Ham and Hams in twenty years' time, or in the event of Jarvis's death – whichever came first – when the time capsule/cake tin was dug up again in front of the world's media.

The hole didn't end up being all that deep as we didn't want to spend too long on it because we weren't sure whether or not digging holes was strictly within the terms of the Golden Parachutes' tenancy agreement. I wrapped the cake tin in two plastic carrier bags.

'To keep the moisture out,' I said.

'And the worms,' Jarvis said. I handed him the wrapped up cake tin and he placed it in the hole and I covered it with soil, replaced the clump of turf and flattened it with the spade. Then we waited for midnight when we would open the champagne and Jarvis would read a short speech he'd prepared.

In twenty years time, or in the event of Jarvis's death – whichever came sooner – whoever it was that dug up the cake tin at the side of the static home would find inside an out of focus photograph of Jarvis from the Calvin sessions, a picture of Princess Diana sitting alone outside the Taj Mahal, a slice of Christmas cake that was already in the tin when Jarvis borrowed it, a CD of 'Livin' La Vida Loca' by Ricky Martin, one of Jarvis's largely fictional acting CVs, some coins, a paperback book called *Even Idiots Can Act*, a packet of gummy bears, a postcard of the Ham and Hams Teahouse on a sunny day with the Union Jack flying outside, a pirated video copy of *Eyes Wide Shut* – a Tom Cruise film that Jarvis didn't like or understand – and a pink plastic Entertainment cheese from a game of Trivial Pursuit.

At ten seconds to midnight we heard a crowd of people counting down from ten to Happy New Year! over by the man-made lake, until their voices were drowned out by the sound of the start of the Golden Parachutes' fireworks display. Jarvis opened the champagne and began his speech about the new millennium; I could hardly hear him but it contained stuff about how brilliant the new millennium was going to be for the world, but mostly how brilliant it was going to be for him. And then he lifted his plastic flute of iffy champagne, proposed a toast, and at the age of twenty-seven Jarvis Ham had his first ever drink.

Cue soap opera music.

* * *

196

After three plastic flutes of bubbly Jarvis was drunk.

And he wanted more.

There was definitely booze in the static home.

'Sherry and wine and maybe some whisky or gin,' he said, tearing at the roots of a rhododendron shrub like some insane anti-gardener. He was looking for the spare key to the static home that his dad had buried in the dirt in one of the ten or so plant pots that stood guard on the cream stone patio on either side of the front door. Jarvis couldn't remember which pot the key was in and there were soon plants and earth scattered all over the patio and nearby grass: camellias, pansies, evergreens and nevergreens. He eventually found the key buried in the compost beneath a clematis that his dad had planted less than a week earlier.

And then Jarvis was too drunk to get the key in the door. He kept missing the lock, scratching the paintwork, holding the door key really tightly between his thumb and forefinger and putting his face up really close to the door with his tongue sticking out the side of his mouth in concentration as he tried to guide the key into the lock, like he was threading a needle while riding the Coney Island Cyclone during an actual cyclone.

'I can do it. I can *do it*,' he said, when I offered to help. 'There,' he said, finally opening the door and staggering inside.

I climbed the steps that led up from the patio and stood in the doorway and watched Jarvis going through all the fake wood fitted cupboards and cabinets in the kitchen and the lounge. As he crashed about, the static home shook ever so slightly. It became less static. I looked up at the wooden sign above the door and hoped it wouldn't fall onto my head.

Jarvis had once told me that when his dad had bought the static home he'd kept it a secret from his wife until one Sunday afternoon when he'd led her blindfolded up the three concrete steps from the patio to the front door. When he removed the blindfold and Mrs

Ham saw the lounge decorated with balloons and flowers and when she saw the HAMBROSIA sign above the door that her husband had spent hours whittling from a piece of driftwood he'd found on the beach, Jarvis said his mother didn't stop crying for twenty-five minutes.

'Wine!' Jarvis declared, and tried to focus on the label of the half empty or half full – depending on whether you were Jarvis or me – bottle he was holding. '*Is* it wine?' he said. 'I think it's wine.' He pulled the cork out with his teeth, spat it on the carpet like a cowboy or a pirate and took a swig. 'Yes, I think it's wine,' he said. 'Let's go watch the fireworks!'

I groaned. It was a private and almost inaudible groan, and yet it could be heard by other designated drivers celebrating New Year all around the world.

'Come on,' Jarvis said and almost knocked me over as he stumbled back across the lounge and down the steps onto the patio. I shut the door and followed him, as he tripped over de-potted plants and garden chairs and began zigzagging his way through other holiday homes and caravans towards the man-made lake and the bangs and booms of the fireworks and the woos and aahhs of the people down below watching them, swigging from the wine bottle and singing 'Livin' La Vida Loca' at the top of his voice as he went. And the amazing thing was that after drinking just a few glasses of alcohol Jarvis's normally out of tune singing voice had somehow miraculously tuned itself. On the last day of the old millennium, as the sky was lit with colourful gunpowder and noise, Jarvis Ham sang like an angel.

No, of course he didn't. If anything his singing was worse. Like a bag of cats on heat being thrown off a bridge.

* * *

On our short but meandering and noisy journey to the boating lake I had to stop Jarvis from cracking his head open by diving into the waterless swimming pool and from going onto the Astroturf for a game of bowls. I had to wrestle a massive bishop from his hands and return it to the giant chessboard and apologise to an elderly man who'd come out on the doorstep of his static home to tell us he was trying to sleep. 'It's new year!' Jarvis shouted at him.

Then as we were almost at the lake, Jarvis suddenly broke into a run. He ran like people say girls run. I kept to a walking pace, following behind, sometimes taking the exact same zigzag route as him. As though Jarvis knew where the mines were.

It was unusual for Jarvis to be in control of the journey. To be his passenger. The one behind the driver. It made a change, a sometimes pleasant one: the sight of Jarvis staggering drunkenly through the holiday and retirement village wavering from side to side like a defective shopping trolley, singing the songs of Ricky Martin while the sky exploded with pyrotechnics, was comically spectacular.

When Jarvis reached the small boathouse by the lake a security guard put his hand out and asked us where we thought we might be going. Jarvis said that he didn't know where we thought we *might* be going but he knew where we *were* going, which was to watch the fireworks and celebrate the start of a new thousand years and he offered the security guard a swig of his wine. The security guard told us it was residents only and Jarvis said he was a resident and offered him the wine bottle again.

The security guard then asked us to leave and Jarvis said no.

So the security guard *told* us to leave and Jarvis still refused.

I apologised on Jarvis's behalf, explaining that he hadn't really drunk alcohol before and just as I'd calmed the whole situation down Jarvis said,

'It's fucking new year!' He said it in a way that was both celebratory and at the same time threatening. The security guard told us that we'd definitely have to leave.

'Now,' he said.

'My mother is ill!' Jarvis shouted completely out of any known context and then he was back to, 'It's fucking new year!' again. It was the first time I'd really heard Jarvis swear. The new millennium was only ten minutes old and it was already certainly turning out to be one for debuts. And then Jarvis stepped drunkenly backwards, momentum took over and he tripped over a mooring rope falling flat on his back just as an off course rocket landed on one of the yachts. When I'd helped him back up onto his feet again the sails of the yacht were on fire. Happy New Year.

All the way back to the car Jarvis treated me to a few tracks from *20 Greatest Drunk Hits Volume 1*.

'You're My Best Friend'.

'I Fucking Love You'.

'Nobody Likes Me'.

'I'm Hungry'.

'What Does it All Mean?'

'I Hate My Life'.

And so on.

I opened the back door of the car, thanking God that I'd bought a four-door vehicle and stood to one side to let Jarvis fall in and onto the back seat and then somebody flicked his standby switch.

I went back to HAMBROSIA to tidy up the plants and garden furniture and collect the fork and the spade. I picked up the empty cardboard box, flattened it and put it in a nearby bin and went back to the car where Jarvis was fast asleep, snoring and dribbling like a very weird baby.

I put the garden tools in the boot – opening and shutting it as quietly as possible – I climbed into the driver's seat and shut the door equally quietly, I started the engine and drove home.

All the way back the sky was lit up like God's Spirograph. It was 1am but fireworks were still going off all over Devon and beyond, and, from where I was viewing them, there appeared to be a spectacular fireworks display over Buckfast Abbey – home of the famous tonic wine manufacturing Benedictine monks, possibly high on some of their own supply.

Aside from his snoring Jarvis was silent all the way home. Until I switched the engine off outside the Ham and Hams and he woke up. And then he threw up.

'I'm sorry, I'm sorry,' he kept saying between retches. I got out of the car and opened the back door, narrowly avoiding a tidal wave of foul smelling Tollinger and warm – let's call it mulled – red wine.

'I'm sorry, I'm sorry,' Jarvis said and I had the feeling he wasn't apologising to me but to himself. He was crying now. Sobbing. He managed to haul himself out of the car, which I was now going to have to pay somebody to steal and set fire to because I would never get the smell out of the seats. He puked once more, then stood taking in deep breaths for a moment before walking off like a man on a mission. He opened the gate at the side of the Ham and Hams and I followed him up the path to the front door of the cottage at the back of the Ham and Hams Teahouse where the Ham family lived. I stood and waited for Jarvis to once again struggle with getting a key into a lock. When he managed to open the door he turned and looked at me.

'Happy New Year Jarvis,' I said, looking at his face all covered in snot and tears and sick. 'I won't kiss you if that's all right.'

'Fuck off,' he said. He went inside, shut the door behind him and I went back to my car and drove home.

End credits.

Closing music.

If you have been affected by any of the issues raised in this day of Jarvis Ham's life, you can contact our helpline on 555 blah blah blah blah blah blah etc.

LLOYD MORLEIGH

It hadn't all been doom and gloom for the police hunting the Breakfast Killer. During their fingertip search for a weapon after the fourth Mister Breakfast attack, the police had found traces of DNA, a lot of DNA actually, probably a bit too much.

The Mister Breakfast car park where Mark Halwell had gargled his last blood filled breath was an occasional dogging venue. What the police had was a DNA smorgasbord that led to them arresting, questioning and releasing without charge two men who were on the sex offenders' register and one member of their own team who probably should have been on it. They had a lot of unidentified spunk to sort through before it was all eliminated as having nothing to do with the murder. They were left with one DNA sample that was unaccounted for. A small trace of blood found on Mark Halwell's clothing that wasn't his own. This unidentified piece of DNA told the police one thing: they were looking for either a first offender or someone who just hadn't been caught yet.

Still, with every new crime the Breakfast Killer committed it stood to reason that they'd have more chance of catching him. Aside from upping his ante from GBH to murder the Breakfast Killer seemed to be sticking to a fairly strict modus operandi. So far he'd struck at night at a branch of the same roadside restaurant chain in a relatively small area of the South West of England, and the pins in the map on the wall of the incident room seemed to be forming a path that was heading in a definite North East direction.

There were 183 Mister Breakfast restaurants in the United Kingdom when the Breakfast Killer first struck. A combination of poor management, overpriced and undercooked meals, competition from supermarket chains and fast food giants and the bad publicity from the attacks meant that by the time of the second fatal attack there were 112. Ninety-two of these were in England and eighteen were in the South West of the country. Of these eighteen seven were on the route mapped out by the pins on the map in the police incident room.

The police ruled out those restaurants that were still open but where the Breakfast Killer had already struck. This left four Mister Breakfasts where they decided the next attack was most likely to take place. And because so far all the attacks had taken place at night on the First of September, as long as the killer continued to be a creature of habit, the police could make an educated guess as to the day, date and one of four possible venues for the next attack. All they needed to do was be there and stop him.

PC Danny Buss was one of four police officers that volunteered to work undercover at a Mister Breakfast on that first night of September 2010. He put on the stupid hat and uniform, with its Mister Breakfast badge – I'd worked there for nearly a year and never got to wear one of those. It really was one law for us one law for them – and he spent the night showing customers to their tables, giving them menus and taking their meal orders in the Mister Breakfast that was on the A303 just past Stonehenge.

He was hardly rushed off his feet. Every Mister Breakfast in the country was practically deserted at night. People were scared. They didn't want to risk being the Breakfast Killer's next victim. The food just wasn't that good.

'At 9.15pm,' PC Buss said, 'an IC1 male carrying a large darkly coloured – either black or dark blue – backpack entered the restaurant where he waited to be seated by the wait to be seated sign. I showed him to a table, he put the backpack on the floor between his feet. I gave him a menu and asked him if he wanted something to drink. The man ordered a pot of English Breakfast tea.' PC Buss flicked through the pages of his notebook, 'Which I thought was unusual as it was night-time.'

'At 9.21pm,' PC Buss continued, 'I took the pot of tea over to the gentleman's table and asked him whether he'd care to order something to eat. He said no and that he was waiting for someone.'

PC Buss was standing by the side of the A303 just past Stonehenge reading a statement to a group of television cameras and newspaper reporters holding outstretched microphones and Dictaphones. Behind him to his right, about fifty yards in the distance, there was a flurry of police and forensics activity outside the Mister Breakfast where he'd worked undercover the night before.

'At 9.47pm I made a note that the gentleman in question was taking an unusual amount of interest in the other customers who came in and out of the restaurant,' he flicked through the pages of his notebook again, 'of which there had been six. I continued to observe the gentleman and at 10pm I asked again whether he would like something to eat and offered him a refill for his teapot. He declined and reiterated that he was waiting for someone.'

PC Buss glanced back at the crime scene hubbub he was missing out on while he was stuck here talking to these journalists.

'At 10.35pm I attempted to engage the gentleman in small talk. I enquired whom it was he was waiting for. He seemed very reluctant to tell me and said only that he was waiting for "someone". I then became aware of an object, possibly a length of pipe, in the gentleman's backpack which was now open on the floor beneath the gentleman's feet.' PC Buss paused and turned a page in his notebook. 'It was at this point I radioed that I may require backup.'

PC Buss cleared his throat and took another quick glance back at the crime scene in the distance. In spite of the composure with which he was delivering his statement to the press, PC Buss had the look of somebody in the midst of an anxiety attack. When the statement was read and the cameras were switched off he looked like he'd either burst into tears or walk out into the traffic hurtling by on the busy A303.

'At 10.49pm the headlights of a vehicle driving into the car park shone across the restaurant window and appeared to attract the gentleman's attention. I observed as he zipped up his backpack and proceeded to walk towards the exit. He opened the door and stepped outside. I put in a further call for immediate backup and followed the gentleman through the restaurant exit.' PC Buss flicked a page in his notebook back and then forward again. 'I followed behind the gentleman as he proceeded to walk in the direction of a white Volkswagen Golf, parked at the far end of the restaurant car park. I am unclear as to the exact time but as the gentleman approached what I presumed to be the car's driver – an IC1 male in his early thirties – the gentleman unzipped his backpack and reached inside for what I understood to be a weapon.' PC Buss closed his notebook. 'It was at this point that I arrested him.'

PC Buss had handcuffed his suspect and searched him for concealed weapons. He'd opened his jacket and found he was wearing underneath a faded Mister Breakfast souvenir t-shirt with its slogan 'I Got My Fill at Mister Breakfast'. In the pocket of the jacket he found a wallet with a bankcard inside with the name Gilles Garnier on. PC Buss asked the suspect if this was his name. The suspect nodded. PC Buss led Gilles Garnier back into the Mister Breakfast and sat him down at the same table where he'd earlier served him tea and he waited for assistance to arrive.

While PC Buss waited he searched the backpack and found an 8-inch piece of scaffolding pole and a folded up road map of the South West of England with all the Mister Breakfast restaurants marked on. At every restaurant where the Breakfast Killer had attacked there was an x drawn on in red felt tip pen. PC Buss also found a magazine called *Weapons to Kill People With*, a Charles Manson action figure, a Sharpie pen, and a pack of twenty-five trading cards with pictures of the world's most prolific serial killers on the front and a list of their crimes and the details of their victims on the back.

Further police officers arrived and Gilles Garnier was put into the back of a car and taken away for questioning. PC Buss sat beside him in the police car: both exhilarated and drained, and still wearing his stupid Mister Breakfast hat.

In the morning, after a long night of questioning, Gilles Garnier's backpack was returned to him. He was asked to check the bag's contents and to sign a form acknowledging that everything was still there. He confirmed that nothing was missing: the map, the magazine, the Sharpie, the action figure, the scaff pole – which turned out to be made of plastic, it was curved in the middle and had the words *Life size Cluedo Weapons ©Waddingtons* printed on the side – and the pack of trading cards. Had the police looked closer at the trading cards they would have found a card with a sketched drawing of a wolf faced man, a French serial killer who was convicted of being a werewolf and burned at the stake in 1573. Above his picture they would have seen the name Gilles Garnier.

Paul Jotz had changed his name by Deed Poll five years ago. He had a morbid curiosity with death and tragedy. He had pen pals on death row in America and wrote to them using the pseudonym Paula Jotz. He collected murderabilia and had a large collection of horror DVDs. But he was always on the lookout for something more.

Using the same set of statistics and methods of deduction as the police had used to place PC Buss undercover to catch a monster, Gilles Garnier/Paul Jotz had gone to the Mister Breakfast on the A303 just past Stonehenge hoping to meet one. He didn't really know what it was he would do if the Breakfast Killer had turned up. Asked for his autograph on the plastic scaff pole with the Sharpie perhaps. Or got him to pose for a photograph to go on his serial killer groupie Facebook page.

Whatever.

The Breakfast Killer had his first fan.

Garnier/Paul Jotz was charged with wasting police time and leaving a hotel or restaurant or similar establishment without paying for the service – namely, one pot of English Breakfast tea – and he was released.

Shortly after Garnier/Jotz's arrest, before he'd been fingerprinted or had his belt and shoelaces confiscated, the Breakfast Killer arrived at the Mister Breakfast on the A303 just past Stonehenge, and claimed Lloyd Morleigh, the chef, as his fifth victim.

Gilles Garnier would be kicking himself almost as much as PC Buss for having missed it.

* * *

For the first two weeks of the new millennium Jarvis was hung-over. He would never drink again. Never ever, he said. He would never drink again. It became his mantra for a while. Every time I saw him he'd say it. Just in case I forgot and accidentally took him to a beer festival or bought him a box of liqueur chocolates or a rum baba.

I drove him to two auditions in February. The first one was for The Interesting Looking Agency, an extras agency specialising in actors who were 'different' or 'interesting'. When I picked Jarvis up for the audition he was wearing a white suit, eye shadow and a sweatband. The agency declined putting Jarvis on their books. They said they felt he was trying too hard. Learning from this mistake Jarvis tried a different approach for the second February audition. He turned up fifteen minutes late wearing a t-shirt and jeans and walked into the audition eating a sticky bun and said, 'So, what's this for again?' He didn't get that one either.

On March 30th 2000 Jarvis summoned me to the Ham and Hams. I arrived at five o'clock just as he was flipping over the sign in the door from OPEN to CLOSED. The flag outside was the five ringed flag of the Olympic Movement. I went in and said hello to Jarvis and his dad, who had his back to us washing dishes.

'Tea?' Jarvis's dad asked without turning around. Before I could answer he was drying his hands on a tea towel and picking up a teapot. 'Scones?' he said, and once again, before I could reply he was putting them on a plate. 'Only go to waste,' he said. 'Have a seat.'

I sat down and watched the Hams finish tidying up at the end of their working day, and then Jarvis's dad brought a tray over with a pot of tea, two large scones and accompanying trimmings on. He put them all on the table in front of me.

'Thank you,' I said. 'How's Mrs Ham?'

'Oh, you know,' Jarvis's dad said. I didn't know, but guessed he didn't want to talk about it. He smiled and went back to finish the washing up.

Jarvis came over and sat down opposite me. He reached into the front pocket of his apron and he took out a folded page from a magazine. He opened it up and put it on the table.

'Well,' he said. 'That's it.'

'What is?'

'It's too late.'

'What's too late?'

'I am. From tomorrow I will officially be too old to join the 27 Club.'

It sounded familiar but I wasn't exactly sure what he was talking about. I poured a cup of tea, asked Jarvis if was having one. He shook his head.

'The 27 Club,' Jarvis said. He waved the magazine article in the air to somehow make things clearer. 'Rock stars who died when they were twenty-seven years old. There's a club.' Jarvis started listing all the members of the 27 Club and the cause of their demise. 'Jimi Hendrix choked on his own vomit. Jim Morrison. Died in a bath. Janis Joplin overdosed on heroin. Brian Jones …' Jarvis looked at the magazine article, he clearly didn't know who half these people were, '… from the Rolling Stones, drowned in a swimming pool. Kurt Cobain shot himself, Robert Johnson was poisoned … there are loads more.'

And he carried on reading out from his magazine list of dead rock and blues legends who died when they were twenty-seven.

'Rudy Lewis, drug overdose. Dickie Pride, another overdose, there are a lot of overdoses. Ron "Pigpen" McKernan.'

And on he went. Over thirty dead rock and blues musicians, I mean, it was fascinating but I just wanted to eat my scones. I didn't give a shit about rock and blues, I was thinking about jam and cream. Jarvis could see that I wasn't really getting what it was he was trying to tell me.

'I'm *twenty-eight* tomorrow,' he said. 'I'll be ineligible.'

He gave me a wide-eyed stare until the penny dropped and I understood.

'But you're not a rock star,' I said, focusing on pedantry rather than finding his disappointment at not being dead anything out of the ordinary. I was used to this sort of nonsense from Jarvis.

'That's not the point,' he said. 'I couldn't be a member if I wanted to be now.' He did actually seem quite upset by it. The bonkers idiot. 'I want to leave a beautiful corpse,' he said, and I literally had to pinch myself underneath the table to stop myself from responding to that one with a wisecrack and a snare drum.

'You could always kill yourself.' I said.

'What?'

I looked at the clock on the wall.

'You've got about six and a half hours. Throw yourself under a bus. You'll still get in.'

'Don't be stupid,' he said. 'I'm never going to die famous am I?'

'You could start a new club,' I said.

'What?'

'The twenty-eight club, twenty-nine, thirty, it's up to you. Probably don't wait too long though.' I filled my mouth with scone. My God, it tasted good. I was in total agreement with Boy George. If it came from the Ham and Hams on a tray with scones, I'd much rather have a cup of tea.

'There's something else,' Jarvis said.

'Mmm mmm,' I said and added another layer of jam to the second scone.

'I've been thinking about it a lot.'

'Yes,' I said. I wasn't listening.

'All these failed auditions.'

'Mmmm hmmm.'

'I'm afraid I might have to let you go.'

'Go where?' I said through a mouthful of scone, boiled sugar and clotted dairy.

'I don't want you to be my manager any more.'

This was a surprise.

Mainly because up until that very moment, I hadn't realised I was his manager.

PART TWO

HAM ALONE

Finding out I was no longer Jarvis's manager less than a second before I discovered that I was his manager and then ending up not being his manager was hard to get my head round.

So I didn't bother.

Without realising how trapped I'd been I was suddenly incredibly aware of how free I was. I started seeing some of my other friends. Going out at the weekends. Enjoying myself.

I met a girl in a bar in Exeter. I drove the forty odd miles there and forty odd miles back to bring her to my flat and then drop her home again. She sat in the front of the car.

Driving back after dropping her home one Sunday evening, a truck went into the back of my silver Vauxhall Omega Elite. The car was a complete write off and it was towed away for scrap. The truck driver had done me a favour. I'd never quite managed to get rid of the smell of Jarvis's sick. I'd had the car valeted and steam cleaned and I'd filled it with a forest of tree shaped air fresheners, but just as I thought the smell had gone, it would reappear. My girlfriend would notice it when she got in the car after I'd grown used to it – hanging around like a bad smell.

While I was waiting for the insurance money to come through I took the bus to work. To get to the bus stop I had to walk along Fore

Street. I'd walk past 123 Fore Street, stopping in to buy a newspaper, I'd pass the two estate agents: sometimes I'd pause to look in the window and see what was for sale. I'd walk on past *Mary*, it wouldn't be open yet but sometimes Mary would be sitting in one of the hydraulic chairs reading a magazine or eating a croissant from next door. I'd poke my head in the door of the Ham and Hams and say hello to Jarvis and his dad. They'd be preparing food for the day, Jarvis slicing bread and his dad icing an elaborate cake. I wouldn't stop to talk; I had to catch the bus I'd say.

Later in the day I'd walk along Fore Street in the other direction on my way home after work. Past the Ham and Hams, which was closed by then and I'd look in the window of *Mary*, at the women with their heads stuck in the astronaut helmets. Sue wasn't there. She was long gone. Swam back to Atlantis with her Italian lifeguard boyfriend. I'd stop and take another look in the estate agents window. I'd long since moved away from Ugly Park into a nice flat in the village, but like Jarvis, I really didn't want to live here for my whole life.

On Fridays I'd maybe buy a pizza and a bottle of wine from 123 Fore Street and take them home to watch TV with my lovely new girlfriend who sometimes came over from Exeter to stay the weekend with me.

Some mornings if I'd overslept or if I was going to be late for work I'd just tap on the window of the Ham and Hams or wave as I ran past. And then after a while, if Jarvis was looking the other way as I went by, I didn't put my head in to say hello or try to attract his attention with a wave or a knock on the window. Some more time passed and I found myself crossing over to the other side of the road so that he wouldn't see me.

The insurance money finally came in from the written off Vauxhall and I bought a red Mini Cooper. I think I'd subconsciously chosen a small car just in case Jarvis changed his mind about me being his manager. If he did change his mind he was going to have to stop cabbing me at least, or have a cramped back-seat ride to his auditions.

For a while I'd drive the Mini along Fore Street on the way to work. I wouldn't honk the horn as I went by or slow down so Jarvis could see me. Soon after that I started taking a different slightly longer route to work, completely bypassing Fore Street altogether.

Then I got a new job in Exeter writing funny church signs and jokes for Christmas crackers and Chinese food. It seemed a long way to drive to and from every day and I moved in with my girl-friend in Exeter during the week and came back to the village at weekends. I hardly saw Jarvis at all. Soon people would be asking me, 'How's Jarvis?' and I'd be saying 'Jarvis who?'

* * *

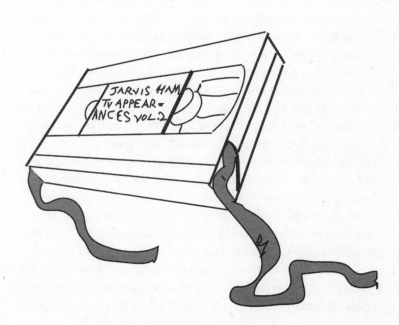

The noughties were an interesting time for fame junkies. It was the golden age of reality television. So many new drugs. So many opportunities to get your fix.

Jarvis wrote a lot of letters to television production companies to tell them why he would be ideal for their reality shows. The Ham and Hams Teahouse needed a makeover he told them. They should send their makeover team round and strip its mismatching wallpaper and gut it of all its personality. He told them the postage stamp of garden outside the Ham and Hams needed a makeover too. He sent them a photograph of the garden and also photos of the interior of the Ham and Hams, with all its antiques and nick-nacks that he suggested could be sold at a boot sale or on a TV auction show. He told them his mother was ill in case that might help get him on TV.

Jarvis made copies of all the letters so that he could write follow-up letters when he received no response. He copied those follow-up letters too. There were a lot of them in the old actor's suitcase.

Jarvis applied to be on cooking shows and dating shows. He said he was prepared to lose weight, to get fit or to get even fatter and then lose the weight in a fat camp, whatever they wanted. He wrote to tell them how he'd love to be stranded on a desert island or travel back to Victorian times or live as a caveman. He applied for talent shows, quiz shows and actual million pound games.

Jarvis's audition tape for *Big Brother* did make it onto TV. It was shown at three in the morning on a satellite TV channel nobody ever watched on a reality TV spin-off show called *Hopeless Hopefuls*. It was the only clip on the second of the two videocassettes I found in the suitcase. The tape had been chewed up and broken and I had to sellotape the two ends of tape together to play it.

The date from the camcorder at the bottom left hand corner of Jarvis's *Big Brother* audition clip is 23.10.01. On the tape Jarvis reads a monologue from Shakespeare and does a few of his funny accents and his Tom Cruise impression – *Show me the money! Show me the money!* He talks about how much fun he is and about his acting career and how he was nearly in a boyband and how he always speaks his mind and he talks about the time he met Diana. As he delivers his final appeal to be picked for the show Jarvis stares into the lens of the video camera and says *Please*. Watching the clip, I felt like the mirror in the film *Taxi Driver*.

Or maybe that was just Jarvis's Mohican haircut.

In July 2002 Jarvis sent his annual letter to the BBC about his book of condolence. This time he also made a number of further suggestions for how the BBC should mark the fifth anniversary of Diana's death and how he, Jarvis, should be involved in them.

At Christmas that same year I saw Jarvis in the centre of Exeter. He was sitting in a chair outside a burger bar drinking from a gold-coloured beer can. He was dressed as a gorilla. It looked like the same gorilla suit he'd worn for the Furniture Circus advert eight years earlier. The suit looked like it needed a wash, it was covered in bald patches and there was a hole below the left armpit. Jarvis looked threadbare himself. His hair was thinning and his sideburns were as grey and wiry as Brillo pads. Jarvis drained the beer can, put it into a carrier bag under the chair, picked up the gorilla's head, put it on and stood up. The suit was a tighter fit than the last time I'd seen Jarvis in it. He'd put on a lot of weight. All those fantastic cream teas and cakes I suppose.

I watched him for a bit as he offered leaflets to passing shoppers that none of them accepted, and then I turned and walked back the way I'd come before he could see me.

There wasn't a lot more in the shoebox or in the old brown leather suitcase from that first decade without my hands (however oblivi-ously) on the managerial rudder or on the steering wheel as Jarvis's designated driver. There was a list of people Jarvis didn't like. It included TV chefs, glamour models, reality TV 'stars' (Jarvis's inverted commas), three prominent members of the Royal Family, people on mobile phones and the man who makes the train announcements at Plymouth railway station, *why should he get the role? Has he got any acting experience? NO*, it said next to his name in thick capital letters.

There was this list of things that people had shouted at Jarvis in the street in October 2003:

I found a piece of paper counting all the times a girl had said the word 'like' on a bus journey to Plymouth:

I found this letter Jarvis wrote to Andrew Lloyd Webber in 2006:

> Jarvis Ham
> The Ham and Hams Teahouse
> Fore Street
> Mini Addledford
> Devon

FAO: Sir Andrew Lloyd Webber

20 September 2006

Dear Lord Lloyd Webber,

I enjoyed greatly your recent search for a stage musical star.

I understand you must be a very busy man so I won't take up too much of your time.

I think I am the perfect person for your next search for a star. I have a lot of

experience in stage acting and musical
theatre. It would be more than my dream come
true to appear in one of your productions. I
know that your time is precious so I won't
take up any more of it other than to say
again that this would be my dream come true.
It would also be brilliant for my mother who
is very ill and is in bed. She loves your
programmes and all your songs.

Thank you for your time
Yours faithfully
JARVIS D HAM

And a copy of this book that Jarvis bought on mail order from
America, with the word 'LIES!' written across the cover:

And that was pretty much it.

After avoiding him in Exeter when he was handing out leaflets for free burgers dressed as a gorilla I didn't see Jarvis again for about five years.

And then I saw him on the News.

It was a report about obesity. The reporter was talking about how British people were the most obese people in Europe or something, while they showed a film of overweight people walking along a street. Not their faces, just their torsos. Jarvis was one of them. Even without seeing his face I knew it was him. I saw the same bit of film about another six or seven times. Whenever there was a piece about obesity they dug it out of the library. Jarvis was finally a television star. Filmed from the neck down, just his fat gut in a washed out mustard coloured t-shirt, walking along a high street somewhere to illustrate what a fat country Britain was. It was hardly the sort of TV exposure he'd been hoping for. If he'd seen it I imagined it would have broken his heart. And that was the last time I saw Jarvis until six months ago.

If I'd heard Jarvis's mother's real name for the first time at her wedding ceremony I might have sniggered to myself. Hearing it for the first time at her funeral was not so funny.

Pamela Ham. Pam Ham. I guess that was why she preferred to be known by her middle name of Maria: because of everybody rolling in the aisles on her wedding day.

Nobody else at Jarvis's mum's funeral laughed either. Most of them had heard her name before. It was practically the same guest list for Pam Ham's funeral as it had been at her wedding. I'm sure there's something clever to be said about that.

My God did I feel a bit guilty turning up at the church to see all Mrs Ham's friends and family waiting outside by a sign that said 'George Michael Was Right – You Gotta Have Faith'.

Why didn't everybody just go inside? Why aren't there more obvious rules for funerals? What were we supposed to do? Wait for the hearse and the family to arrive first? Or go in the church and sit down? Is it deceased's family on the left?

Nobody wanted to be the first to enter the church. You don't want to look too keen at a funeral. So there we all were, just standing around outside in front of my stupid sign, until one of the undertakers finally asked us all to go into the church as the cortège would be arriving soon.

Twenty Greatest Church Organ Funeral Hits was playing softly as I looked for a seat as far from the front as possible, although not too close to the back either. Somewhere in the middle, but not too near the aisle in case I tripped one of the pallbearers up or something. I found the most neutral pew in the building and sat down.

The organ music volume increased slightly and the coffin was carried in. Everybody stood. We knew that much at least. Jarvis and his dad followed slowly behind the coffin, along with other members of the family. They sat down at the front of the church and then the rest of us sat down too.

Jarvis had lost a lot of the weight he was carrying when I last saw him in the obesity News clips. He was back to the sort of shape he was in when he was dressed as the gorilla in the shopping centre: obese but not morbidly so. It was the first time I could recall seeing Jarvis in a suit that wasn't yellow or white or gorilla and wearing a tie that wasn't his school tie or one with a piano keyboard down the front. He was wearing black gloves.

Everybody mumbled uncomfortably along with a hymn that sounded improvised, apart from Jarvis, whose voice was loud, out of tune and almost definitely rehearsed. The vicar did his bit about God, followed by Jarvis's dad with a few sad words, and then it was time for the headline act. It would be wrong and unfair to say that for Jarvis this was just another opportunity to be onstage before an audience, but there was something about the eulogy he read out for his mother that made me think he was auditioning for a role of grieving son, and at other moments it was a bit like an Oscar acceptance speech.

And I couldn't help feeling that I'd heard some of it before somewhere else. Later I'd Google the bits I could remember and I got 193,000 hits leading to the speech Princess Diana's brother made at his sister's funeral. I was just thankful that Jarvis didn't finish with a song.

With the exception of a half-mast flag – Alaska with its eight gold stars forming the Big Dipper on a blue background – outside the Ham and Hams Teahouse, the similarities with Diana's funeral ended with Jarvis's plagiarism in the church. A crowd of millions didn't line the streets applauding the hearse and throwing flowers onto its bonnet as it passed. No book of condolence was opened. Not even by Jarvis. There was no candlelit vigil at the Ham and Hams – strange that he should invest so much of himself in the death of somebody he didn't know and yet hardly anything at all for the passing of his own mother. There were no soldiers or police motorbikes. A pop star didn't rewrite the lyrics to one of his pop songs and sing it in the church, and the UK suicide rate of women in their early sixties was largely unaffected.

Back at the Ham and Hams after the funeral Jarvis's dad had laid on an array of cakes fit for a princess though, even if the Ham and Hams Teahouse itself had seen far better days. Jarvis's dad had been too busy to run it as efficiently as usual and look after his sick wife as well. There was dust on the glass of the floor to ceiling cake cabinet, washing up was unwashed up in the sink, the pictures on the walls were wonky, the windows needed cleaning, bulbs needed changing in some of the far from standard lamps and there were crumbs on the floor and in the grooves of the mismatched furniture.

The rest of Fore Street was partially closed for the day. Mary and her staff were all at the wake. The husband and wife who'd just taken over 123 Fore Street were there too, and the apple-faced men from the estate agents came in for a couple of glasses of wine and to pay their respects.

At the wake I found it difficult to hold a conversation with Jarvis. There was so much for us to catch up on, but it felt like we were strangers and I was soon resorting to small talk just to find something to fill the silence.

'Your dad was saying, at least she wasn't in any pain,' I said. 'At the end. And in her sleep. That's something I suppose.'

'She was in a lot of pain,' Jarvis said. 'A *lot* of pain.'

'Oh, sorry, your dad was say …'

'She died in agony if you really want to know the truth. It took a long time as well. And she was awake. Wide awake.' Jarvis looked at the people gathered in for his mother's wake. 'I hope my death is sudden,' he said, gesturing with his wine glass towards the dozen or so people in the teahouse and splashing red wine onto the floor. 'Nobody goes to your funeral if your death is expected.'

I wanted to find a way out of this conversation. 'It was a nice service,' I said. And having run out of post funeral clichés, I asked a dumb question. Do you remember when I said that there would be a point when you'd feel stupid for having felt sorry for Jarvis? This is that time.

'Where were you when you heard?' I said.

'At home,' he said.

'Oh.'

'Wanking.'

That's what I thought he said. Although obviously I'd misheard him.

'Was it busy? When you heard?'

'Not *working*,' Jarvis said.

If it had ended there it wouldn't have been quite so bad. He was probably in shock after all. Grieving the death of his mother. He didn't know what he was saying. He'd been drinking.

It didn't end there.

'And do you know what?' he said.

'What?' Why did I have to ask?

'After I heard, I put the phone down and then I had to decide. What do I do now?'

And Jarvis went on to tell me how he was powerless to do anything to help his mother now. She was gone. He couldn't save her life or say goodbye or anything. There was really nothing he could do for her. And so he finished masturbating.

After a couple of hours people started to leave the wake, kissing each other and shaking hands and promising to see more of each other and not wait until such a sad occasion to bring them together again. They wouldn't of course. Somebody would have to die.

Soon there were just four of us left in the Ham and Hams. Me, Jarvis, one of his aunts and Jarvis's dad who was already clearing up, washing cups and saucers and plates. Before he went to bed he'd clear up all the crumbs, clean the windows, wipe the dust off the big tall glass cabinet and change the light bulbs.

The Ham and Hams would rise again.

Like a soufflé from the ashes.

Jarvis asked me if I'd give him a lift to the Golden Parachutes Holiday and Retirement Village. He said he didn't want to stay at home because he was too upset and his aunt was staying in his room so it made sense for him to sleep elsewhere. Seeing as how I had to drive past the retirement village on my way home it was difficult to say no.

We said goodbye to his dad and his aunt and walked to my latest car – a white Nissan Micra – and just for old times' sake Jarvis climbed into the back and fell asleep all the way home.

On the way I thought about something Jarvis's dad had told me at the wake. He said that when his wife was admitted to hospital for the final time, he'd spent a lot of time after work at the hospital sitting beside her bed, feeding her her dinner and reading the gossip from magazines to her. One evening he came back from visiting his wife at the hospital and he found Jarvis at home at the bottom of the stairs, semiconscious and with a bloody nose. He'd fallen down the stairs.

And then a week or so later Jarvis's dad had come back from the hospital earlier than usual. He'd found Jarvis at the foot of the stairs again, scratching the inside of his nostril with a butter knife to make his nose bleed: just before faking a fall down the stairs.

'I think he was jealous,' Jarvis's dad said.

'Of his *mother*?' I said, and his father screwed his face up, bit his bottom lip, and nodded.

Jarvis slept the whole way back from the wake. As soon as I switched the engine off at the Golden Parachutes he woke up.

'Are we here?' he said.

'Yes. I don't suppose I could quickly use the toilet?' I asked him.

We walked to the Hams' static home, Jarvis opened the door and we went inside. The lounge looked the same as when I'd last seen it. The colours had maybe faded a bit, the shag pile was not as deep and there was a layer of dust on all the fitted fake wood surfaces. Once Jarvis's dad had finished doing the dishes at the Ham and Hams he'd probably come out here next and give everything a good clean, Hoover the carpet and then I guess he'd put it up for sale.

When I came out of the toilet and back into the lounge Jarvis wasn't there. Aside from the bathroom and combined lounge and kitchen there were two bedrooms. One of the bedroom doors was slightly ajar. Through the gap I saw Jarvis; he was on his knees by the bed. The old actor's suitcase his dad had bought him for his eighteenth birthday was open on the floor in front of him. I watched as Jarvis put something inside the case, closed it and locked it with a large padlock. I called out his name and through the gap between the bedroom door and the doorframe I saw him hurriedly push the suitcase under the bed.

I stepped back away from the door. I didn't want him to think I was spying on him. When he came out into the lounge he had the expression of a teenage boy who'd just been caught by his parents with a porn mag. It was a look that reminded me of what he'd said about the night he'd heard about his mother's death and I suddenly really quite desperately wanted to leave.

Outside the static home I said goodbye to Jarvis and I wrote my phone number on the back of one of my overly subtle business cards and hoped that he wouldn't actually ring me.

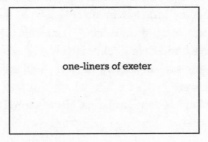

one-liners of exeter

Six days later Jarvis called.

'It's a fantastic opportunity,' he was saying.

'Who is it?' my girlfriend called out from the kitchen. It was a Thursday evening, she was cooking pasta, I was watching TV when the phone had rung.

'Jarvis,' I called back to my girlfriend. 'What is?' I said into the phone.

'It's something to do with carbon footprints,' Jarvis said. 'Who was that you were talking to?'

'My girlfriend. Go on.'

'The airlines have to have a certain amount of passengers on their aeroplanes. If they haven't got enough passengers they're fined.'

'I still don't really understand,' I said.

Jarvis read out the advert he'd seen in the newspaper, "Extras wanted. Free flights! Actors required immediately to fly to Ireland and return to Exeter Airport." I could play an airline passenger. That's well within my range. And you get paid. Two hundred and forty pounds.'

'Fantastic,' I said. I tried to seem enthusiastic but sounded more sarcastic. I was tired and hungry, my girlfriend was dishing up in the kitchen, the wine was open and we had a DVD on pause ready to go.

'The thing is,' Jarvis said, 'I could do with a lift to the airport.'

My silence spoke volumes.

'It won't take long,' Jarvis said. 'You just have to drop me at the airport', and then he added as an afterthought, as though it was a tiny unimportant insignificant detail, 'And wait for me to fly to Ireland and back.' And then one more tiny irrelevant detail, 'And then drop me home again afterwards. You could even go home in between if you want.'

'That's very kind of you. But Jarvis, I have a job,' I said.

'It's on Saturday.'

'But ...'

'Just this once.'

I could have just told him to get a taxi. Wasn't there some sort of shuttle bus? Couldn't his dad drive him? It was only fifty miles or so, couldn't he walk? Any of those things I could have said. But I felt sorry for the big balloon-headed idiot. His mother had just died.

I knew it wouldn't be just once. I knew that soon I'd be driving him to auditions and casting calls again. I'd get up so soon after I'd just gone to bed that I might as well have stayed up so I could go and pick him up and drive him to Bristol for the open auditions of a TV talent show. I'd drop him off and go and wait in the car park for him. I'd read a book or answer some work emails while I waited four or five hours for Jarvis to reach the front of the audition queue so that he could barely open his mouth before someone shouted *Next!* And then I'd drive him home again, sulking all the way, only to do it all over again at the Cardiff heats for the same show a week later.

I'd drive Jarvis to auditions for parts in amateur productions of plays and musicals he didn't have a hope in hell of getting. I'd drive him into Plymouth where he'd dress up in a huge rubber tooth suit to hand out leaflets for a dental surgery. Two hours later I'd get a phone call at work and I'd have to drive back to Plymouth to pick him up and take him to the same dentist he was handing out leaflets for after some kids had pushed him over in his tooth suit, causing him to ironically chip his tooth.

I'd even take Jarvis swimming again: driving even further away from home in search of a pool where they didn't think we were a couple of nonces. And what fun we'd have. There'd be that time when somebody broke into his locker while we were in the pool and stole all his clothes and I had to walk with him to the car park shivering to death in his trunks, wrapped in my towel. And the time when someone stole his shoes and his flip-flops and he had to walk to the car wearing the blue polythene overshoes from the changing room.

Just when I thought I was out, Jarvis Ham pulls me back in.

Yes okay, I'd drive him to the airport.

When I picked him up outside the Ham and Hams, to the untrained eye Jarvis was dressed fairly normally: cream trousers, navy golfer jacket, comfortable shoes and a green polo shirt. But I knew he was dressed as an airline passenger. It was a costume. The overnight bag he was carrying was full of screwed up newspaper. Jarvis had probably been up half the night practising his airline passenger looks and watching films about airports.

Observing his short walk to the car I could see Jarvis had a different walk to his usual ungainly lollop. It was his airline passenger's walk. Jarvis climbed into the back of the car. It seemed I would be playing my usual role of mini cab driver.

'Where to sir?' I said.

'Ho ho,' Jarvis said, filling the car with his boozy breath (it was 5am).

In 2007 Jarvis had flown to Paris on the tenth anniversary of Princess Diana's death. He'd visited the Ritz Hotel and walked in and out through the same revolving doors he'd watched Diana walk through a hundred times or more on video. He took a taxi to the road tunnel beneath the Place de l'Alma and was stopped by police as he entered the busy underpass and started walking down towards the fatal thirteenth pillar – a number the more superstitious conspiracy theorists thought was somehow significant – to leave a bouquet of flowers. Turned back from the tunnel by the police, Jarvis left his flowers instead at the foot of the Flamme de la Liberté, the gold leaf covered life-size replica of the flame at the end of the torch held by the Statue of Liberty in New York that had been adopted by mourners and tourists as their unofficial Diana memorial. And then he slept in Charles de Gaulle Airport until his flight back home again.

The trip to Ireland as a pretend passenger would be the second time Jarvis had been on a plane. I watched him go through to the departure gate and I walked back to the car and started driving home to get a bit of work done until it was time to drive back to the airport again to pick him up. I was almost home when I saw the sign for the Golden Parachutes and almost without thinking I turned off and drove there instead. It was that suitcase. It had been bothering me.

The case had never been locked in the past, and there was something about the way Jarvis had reacted when he thought I might have caught him locking it that made me want to know why he was locking it.

It was a long way to drive back to my house, I told myself. By the time I got there it would almost be time to leave for the airport again. That's what I told myself. Just pull in at the retirement village and wait there for a while instead. While I was there, I said to myself, I might as well look in the plant pots outside HAMBROSIA to see if the spare key was still there.

It was.

I found the key buried under the same clematis where Jarvis had found it more than ten years previously. The clematis was dead and there was an empty crisp packet and some fox shit in the pot with it but I'm pretty sure it was the same plant. Carefully avoiding the fox shit I picked the key out, and once I'd gone that far I might as well open the door.

My heart was racing. I was definitely doing something wrong. I opened the door slowly. I called out hello. What my next words would have been if someone had answered I had no idea. Luckily nobody answered.

I stepped inside. I checked the kitchen and the other bedroom first. Trying to think of a story in case I found Jarvis's dad asleep in bed or if I found Jarvis – even though logic told me that I'd just left him at the departure gate for a flight to Ireland. There was nobody home.

This left just the room with the suitcase under the bed. The door was closed and I gave myself two options. Kick it open and rush inside ready for a fight, perhaps in some sort of kung fu or karate stance. Or I could very slowly open the door and say hello again. I went for option number two, and slowly tiptoed into the bedroom, gently hello-ing as I did so.

I went over to the window, pulled the closed curtains slightly apart and checked there was nobody outside. Other than a lone yacht on the fake lake in the distance, waiting for a gust of wind, the man-made coast was clear.

I got down on the floor and slowly lifted the bedspread. I saw the brown suitcase underneath the bed.

I thought I heard a noise coming from the lounge and once again called out hello. No answer.

I reached under the bed and pulled out the case – it was heavier than I'd imagined and I dragged the carpet out with it. I looked at the stickers covering the case: all those Broadway productions and exciting places – India and Japan, New York, Paris and Hollywood. Mocking Jarvis for his life of inertia just like the flags in the garden outside the Ham and Hams. I pushed the button across on the left latch and it popped open. I did the same with the one on the right. It was now just the padlock in the centre that was keeping me out. The words *Create Your Own Combo* © were printed into the metal of the padlock. There were four numbers to choose in the lock's combination. I had something like one in ten thousand chances of getting it right. Without even really thinking about it I turned the numbered wheels round: 1. 2. 3. 4. The lock snapped open.

I don't know what I expected to find in the suitcase. Photographs of Jarvis and me standing next to him with a hole cut out where my head should be or with a big red cross drawn through my face. Maybe a stash of hardcore pornography or some combat clothing and a load of gun magazines. Or Ronnie – Jarvis's ventriloquist's doll, staring accusingly up at me.

What I actually found was a purple scrapbook with not much in it, a couple of videocassettes, an Oscar statue, various notepads, books and other bits of crap, and this shoebox.

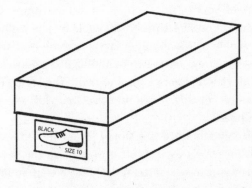

Once I'd started reading Jarvis Ham's diary I found I couldn't stop. Obviously I'd heard about his British Museum birth fifty million times before but I'd never seen the newspaper cutting to prove it wasn't just one of his dad's little white lies. I was part of the throne carrying cast for Jarvis's first acting gig but I'd forgotten all about it. I remembered the Diana poem, but only when I saw it again all those years later.

I read the Jennifer Fer stuff and looked through some of the leaflets and newspaper cuttings advertising auditions and promotion work. I'd been sitting on the bedroom floor with my feet folded under me for so long that when I stood up my legs had gone numb and I had to sit on the bed until the feeling and the ability to walk returned.

I went out into the lounge and put the first volume of Jarvis's TV appearances into the video machine that was built into the fake wood fitted unit like the dashboard stereo of a car. The tape was at the end and I had to rewind it, which seemed to take for ever – ten years of DVDs and already the VHS seemed practically Stone Age.

While the tape was rewinding I looked in some of the cupboards in the lounge. Aside from half a dozen bottles of Jarvis's emergency alcohol I found a pack of cards, a few Catherine Cookson novels and a stack of board games – it was a holiday home after all. I pictured the Hams all sat round the table on the L-shaped sofa playing Scrabble or Monopoly – Jarvis arguing over words that didn't exist or always having to be the banker and sulking if he didn't get Mayfair and Park Lane. I took out the Trivial Pursuit. A pink cheese was missing. It had been replaced with a tiny piece of folded cardboard.

The videotape thudded to a stop. I sat down and watched the clips of Jarvis being mistaken for a woman on the daytime talk show, Jarvis trying to steal focus at the horse racing, and dressed as a gorilla in the furniture ad.

When the video finished I fast-forwarded through the blank tape snow for a while until it was back where it was when I found it and then I realised I was going to be late back at the airport.

I took the videotape out of the machine and put it and everything else back into the old suitcase, trying to remember how it was arranged – which was not at all, just thrown in in no obvious particular chronological order, unless that was an elaborate trick to catch out nosy bastards like me and although everything looked as though it had been dropped randomly into the suitcase from a plane, in actual fact it was all very precisely arranged to appear that way. Spying on people makes you paranoid.

I did my best to put it back the way I found it, padlocked the suitcase and put it under the bed. I rearranged the carpet and put the bedspread back the way I'd found it. I closed the bedroom door and the front door and I put the key back in the pot next to the fox crap and the crisp packet and went to collect Jarvis from the airport.

A week later I returned to the Golden Parachutes. I found the key in the same place, opened the door and called out hello again.

The next time I came I'd definitely make sure I had a prepared story for what I was doing there in case anybody answered.

The more I read of Jarvis's collection of memories the more I felt guilty for having left him to suffer his relentless failure alone for the past ten years. Ten lonely years of not succeeding, trying, trying and trying again, getting back on the horse over and over, even though it kept throwing him off and kicking him while he was on the ground. It must have been hard work picking himself up, dusting himself off and starting all over again without someone to offer a helping hand or at least a bit of moral support and a lift home.

I felt at least partly responsible for what all the years of disappointment must have done to Jarvis.

Maybe I could make it up to him somehow. I was already sorting the contents of the suitcase into vague date and time order in my head. Perhaps I could compile Jarvis's diary for him. He'd love that. He'd forgive my trespass for that. I could put it all into a book and give it to him as a belated fortieth birthday present.

I started putting the diary entries and press clippings into chronological order. Laying stuff out on the floor and moving it around like a sliding plastic tiled word puzzle. Arranging the various publicity photographs of Jarvis by the age he appeared to be in them. On my next trip I'd take the photographs and some of the newspaper cuttings to a photocopy shop and I'd start copying the diary entries into my laptop. It would be like a school project.

One night I was on my way back home from a business meeting and found it impossible to pass by the retirement village without stopping off to do a quick bit of work on Jarvis's diary. I parked the car and walked to the Hams' static home. As I turned the corner at the end of the adjacent row of holiday homes I saw there was a light on in the lounge of the Hams' holiday home. Somebody was standing at the window looking out. I spun round and walked back to the car park, breaking into a jog and finally running all the way back to the car. I drove away hoping Jarvis or his dad or whoever it was hadn't seen me. I convinced myself the light in the lounge would have made it impossible for whoever it was to be able to see out.

When I picked Jarvis up from the airport, and even more so on the many subsequent times when I was driving him to or from another failed audition or near drowning at the swimming pool, I found myself almost starting a conversation about the contents of the suitcase under the bed.

'Did you write a letter to the BBC this year?' I'd start saying, and realise I was talking about something I shouldn't know about and change the subject quickly. Or, 'that was your favourite song in nineteen ninety thre ...' that sort of thing.

I had a lot of questions I wanted to ask Jarvis. I wanted to ask him about Jennifer Fer and about Sue. I wanted to ask him about the *Big Brother* video and the girl on the bus who said the word 'like' 173 times. But I didn't want to spoil the surprise. When I presented Jarvis with his diary, all compiled in the correct order with photographs and an index and an out of focus picture taken by Calvin on the cover, then we could talk about it.

* * *

When the chef was found murdered on the ground next to his white pleated hat it was the final straw for the ailing roadside restaurant chain. It was as though Mister Breakfast himself was dead. The company went into administration and the CEO took an overdose of sleeping pills – becoming the Breakfast Killer's sixth victim.

Only one Mister Breakfast restaurant survived. We were coming up to it now. We weren't far from our final destination but I needed to stop, that's what I told Jarvis: just a quick piss break and maybe a cup of coffee, as I was pretty tired.

The only surviving Mister Breakfast was the one that a celebrity chef had reinvented the menu for as part of a reality TV series. The sausages were now organically farmed, the steak and ale pie was locally sourced and the braised ox cheeks were rosy when a bolt was fired into the ox's free-range head. I'd never been to this Mister Breakfast myself till now, mainly because there was nothing on the absurdly poncy and overpriced menu for vegetarians.

I drove into the busy car park and looked for a space.

'This thing tomorrow?' Jarvis said. 'You don't think I'm too old?'

'Of course not,' I said, our eyes meeting as I checked behind me to reverse into the only car park space left.

Jarvis had been so excited when I'd rung him to tell him how I'd found some acting work for him in London. He'd talked for ages on the phone about how he genuinely thought this really could actually be his big chance.

'Do you think this could be it?' he'd asked me on the phone.

'Sure,' I'd said.

'Brilliant.'

I parked the car and we walked towards the restaurant with its bright new colour scheme and south facing windows sparkling in the sun. The cartoon chef was still on the sign outside, but his welcoming toothy grin was now an insincere Hollywood smile, his droopy moustache had been trimmed and he was wearing a smart white chef jacket over his wife-beater vest. The sausage was still on the end of his fork, but it was free range and organic. Other than in name this place wasn't really a Mister Breakfast at all.

The staff were way too friendly for a start, and there were too many of them. Their uniforms were new and funky, designed by someone else off the telly. The hats weren't stupid enough. The toilets looked and smelled cleaner than the kitchens and eating areas of most of the other now defunct or demolished Mister Breakfasts. It was all just too nice. The celebrity chef had sucked all the personality out of the place.

There were two sets of automatic entrance doors. We went through the first set of doors into what was a sort of foyer area before the Mister Breakfast itself. In the foyer there was a cash machine, a post box, some kind of payphone and Internet gizmo and a few temporary stalls for people to stand behind and sign customers up for credit cards, spa weekends and other crap they hadn't realised they wanted when they got into their cars that day. On the walls there were interactive pictures of lamb chops, roast beef and sausages. If you touched the pictures they made the sounds baa, moo and oink. The celebrity chef said it was important for people to know where the food on their plate came from. Perhaps it would have been more accurate if when you touched the pictures, hideous screams of pointless agonising death filled the restaurant.

Above the entrance to the restaurant there were four clocks showing the times for LONDON, PARIS, MILAN and MADRID. Above each clock in turn were the words: Mister Breakfast, Monsieur Petit Déjeuner, Colazione di Signore and Desayuno de Señor.

I started walking off towards the toilets and asked Jarvis to go ahead and find us a table in the restaurant.

'Shall I order the drinks?' he said as I walked away.

I turned back to see his big idiotic balloon-face looking back at me. I couldn't help feeling bad about what I was going to do. Even though Jarvis was a big balloon-faced idiot he was my big balloon-faced idiot, and I loved him. I think I'm enough in touch with my girlfriend's feminine side to be able to say that.

'Coffee please,' I said. 'Thanks.'

Jarvis went into the restaurant and I walked off in the direction of the toilets. There were three uniformed men near the gents. The first one tried to stop me to sign me up for the RAC and I told him I was already a member.

'Can I interest you in the AA sir?' the second uniformed man said.

'I'm already a member thanks,' I said and walked on by.

The third uniformed salesman was a policeman. He was handing out leaflets appealing for any information that may lead to the arrest of the Breakfast Killer. On the wall behind him there was a larger poster version of the leaflet.

'Good afternoon sir,' he said.

'Afternoon,' I replied, and walked past him and out through the second set of automatic doors back out into the car park.

When I'd finished compiling Jarvis's diary a week ago I returned to the Golden Parachutes one last time and dug up the time capsule. I'd decided Jarvis's diary wouldn't be complete without it. I was going to photocopy some of the contents and then put it all back in the hole at the side of the static home.

I dug up the cake tin, took it out of one carrier bag and then the other. I put the tin on the ground and prised the lid off.

I took out the photograph of Jarvis with his Tom Cruise hairdo. Great days, I thought, great days, even though they really probably weren't. In the tin underneath Jarvis's picture was the photo of Diana sitting alone outside the Taj Mahal, the video of *Eyes Wide Shut* and the Christmas cake that still looked surprisingly edible, but that's what they say about Christmas cake isn't it? It improves with age or something. The 'Livin' La Vida Loca' CD was there – I thought about Jarvis running towards the fireworks singing it, all drunk and happy and out of tune. Jarvis's bogus acting CV was in the tin, there were quite a few failures to be added. The coins were there – how much had they devalued in such a short time?

I took out the inaccurately titled *Even Idiots Can Act* paperback, the gummy bears and the pink Trivial Pursuit cheese – 'I'm going to be the answer to a Triv Entertainment question soon,' Jarvis had once said to me. I held the postcard of the Ham and Hams Teahouse up to the light to see if I could see Jarvis inside, serving tea to a tourist or slicing one of his father's insane and delicious cakes. I couldn't.

There were a few things in the cake tin that weren't there when I'd filled the hole in at the start of the millennium.

This poster:

This name badge:

And right at the bottom of the tin there was a diary.

Like the collection of boot sale junk that I'd been compiling, it wasn't a diary in the conventional sense. It was a plain A5 notebook, similar to the one Jarvis had bought from WH Smith at Plymouth Station when he took a train to Paddington to buy a teddy bear to leave at Kensington Palace. There were only five entries in the notebook. They were more rambling than ever. The pages were written on and scribbled out. Some of it was very hard to read – in so many ways. I've tried my best to transcribe as much of it as I can.

Every entry in the diary is for the First of September.

WH
S

A5 Notebook

9 012938 109282 >

2007

When I got back to Exeter Airport I felt like I didn't really want to go on any longer. I wanted to sit down right where I was in the middle of the airport. All those holidaymakers and businessmen and people who just didn't seem to care. I wished I'd gone into the tunnel. When it was dark and the policemen were gone away. I wish I'd just stood and waited for the end. Waited for a car to hit me. I'd first seen him taking pictures of an actress. She obviously wanted to just be left alone. What was it with these people? Didn't he know what day it was? I just wanted to go home. That was all. I didn't plan to be in a cubicle next to him. There was music playing in the toilets. It was 'She's the One'. The man was washing his hands and singing along with Robbie Williams. When the man left the toilet I came out behind him. I was just going to leave. I was just going home. It felt thrilling in a way I can't understand. His face seemed to burst when it hit the wall. I thought I'd killed him. I didn't mean to kill him. I didn't mean to do anything. I was just going home.

Robbie Williams had told him to do it. You couldn't blame Jarvis for lack of originality. God was the usual scapegoat. But Robbie Williams? Jarvis had got the gender wrong of course. *She's* the One. Still.

The second attack was the fault of the media. Everyone always blames the media. But they fed Jarvis's addiction. They gave him a harder hit of what Miss whatever-her-name-was – I suppose I should find out her name, although it's really not important at the moment – had given Jarvis when she offered him the role of King Tut at primary school. After that first attack in the Mister Breakfast corridor, the newspapers had put Jarvis on the front page. The idiots.

2008

I just wanted to know what it would feel like. To do it deliberately. I want to say the hospital uniform was the thing that made it happen again. But I know that isn't true. I wanted it to be the fault of him working in a hospital, a place where Diana had died and where Mum spends so much of her life, which is hardly a life at all is it? I know it isn't that. It can't be just that. Who would do that just because of the clothes someone was wearing? I should be in a hospital. I know there's something wrong with me. I wanted to go back to the same place where it happened a year ago and see how it felt but it's gone. It's not there any more. And so I had to go further. To a different place that was almost the same really. I used a big spanner that I found in the car. I hit him so hard. And I knew that this time he was dead. And then I found out that he wasn't dead. I felt better about that.

2009

I think I want to be caught now. I want it to stop. If I can hit somebody twice then I am a monster now. If I want to be caught why did I stop myself from being sick until I was far away? I know the police look for DNA. I was wearing my gloves again as well. I don't think I want to be caught at all. I need to be caught. I am scared that I might not be able to stop now.

2010

I hit him over and over again. I hate what I have become. I am disgusting. I don't know if I can stop. I will buy all the newspapers tomorrow and I will count the pages with my name on and cut them out. There will be more than before. I know I'll be pleased about that.

2011

I had to travel a long way this year. I almost turned back. Listen to me, 'I had to travel a long way this year.' Ha ha. How inconvenient. I saw police cars leaving when I got there. The restaurant was closed. There were lights on but there was nobody there. I would have stopped. I was going to go home and stop. But the lights suddenly went off and the chef came out. He had a coat on over his uniform but he'd forgotten to take his chef hat off. He looked funny. I was laughing to myself and even when I hit him I think I was still laughing. It was like I was acting. I was a character in a film.

After the first murder the newspapers gave Jarvis's character a name. By the time he'd killed the chef he had his own fan club. People were talking about him on the television and in six page Sunday magazine articles. There'd been a number of reconstructions of his crimes on television. Someone somewhere was probably writing a book about him and one day there would be a film. Maybe Tom Cruise would be put forward for the lead role. If the character was big enough, if the crimes were brutal enough, why not?

Nobody would remember the names of the victims. Dean Bantham, Shane Prior, Simon Aveton, Mark Halwell and Lloyd Morleigh would soon be forgotten by everyone other than their families and friends. No one would forget the Breakfast Killer.

When he stove Lloyd Morleigh's chef-hatted head in Jarvis was merely a snowball rolling down a hill.

What it actually was that made Jarvis do it I don't really know. Maybe nobody ever would. Fame is not a big enough motive surely. Was it simply all an accident that escalated into something more wilful and premeditated? How far could the drugs analogy be stretched? Had Jarvis tried a bit of GBH in the toilet corridor and wanted something harder? Something even more addictive? More heroiny.

Jarvis didn't really fit the usual profile of a killer. If he had then the police might have caught him by now. Although I'm sure when the same people watching the News with the sound turned down when Mark Halwell's picture appeared on the screen and thanking God the killer had been caught would be saying that they'd guessed it was Jarvis all along.

One thing I kept thinking about – that almost made me laugh – was how when Jarvis was arrested his neighbours and the people who'd known him certainly wouldn't be able to go on the News and say that Jarvis had always kept himself to himself.

The night after I dug up Jarvis's time capsule I rang the Pizza Hut by the leisure centre and asked to speak to Jennifer. My heart was thumping as I waited to hear her voice. I heard people in the pizza restaurant singing happy birthday to either Sharon or Alan and then cheering after either Sharon or Alan had presumably blown out the candles on their birthday cake. I heard the volume of the music playing in the restaurant go back up, it was a boyband ballad. Not 543212345, but let's just pretend it was for the sake of the story.

'Hello?'

When I heard her voice at the other end of the line I was so relieved that I couldn't think of anything to say. I should have realised when the person who'd answered the phone had gone away to get Jennifer rather than telling me that she hadn't been in for a while and nobody knew where she was – that should have been a clue that she was all right. But I wasn't thinking straight. I had a lot on my mind.

I wanted to ask her about her name badge and if she knew how it came to end up in a cake tin buried at the Golden Parachutes Holiday and Retirement Village. But that would lead to so many questions I couldn't answer for her yet. I was just glad to hear Jennifer's voice, all alive and lovely and everything. What had she ever seen in Jarvis?

There was an awkward silence between us, similar to the one in the leisure centre car park and if I hadn't apologised six or seven times for disturbing her and hung up the phone then I would definitely have fallen in love with her.

I didn't bother ringing to check if Jarvis had murdered 543212345. I figured I would have heard about that. And besides, if Jarvis's experience was anything to go by, trying to get through to their management on the phone was a nightmare.

I was going to say that there was one thing left about all of this that was bothering me, one thing that I couldn't quite understand or make sense of, but that's a ridiculous understatement. I don't understand any of it. But there was one particular detail I couldn't work out, and that was how Jarvis had managed to get to all those roadside restaurants. Every year they got further and further away from his home.

Jarvis's dad cleared that up for me a couple of days ago when he was telling me about how he was thinking of selling the holiday home.

'Maria never really liked it there,' he said. 'And it's only Jarvis who really uses it at all now.' He stopped talking to rub harder on a stubborn smudge on the corner of the baking tray he was washing. 'Although even Jarvis hardly ever goes there either now. Not as much as before. He was virtually living there last year.'

I said to Jarvis's dad that it must have been hard for him, looking after his wife and running the teahouse all on his own while Jarvis was at the holiday home. It seemed a selfish thing to do to his parents.

'Oh no,' Jarvis's dad said. 'Jarvis was still here.' He rubbed the washing up sponge even harder into the stubborn baking tray smudge until it finally disappeared. 'That's got it,' he said. 'He commuted.'

'Commuted?' I said.

'Park and ride.'

'Park and … I don't understand.' I walked nearer to Jarvis's dad. 'Park what and ride?'

'His car. He drove to the park and ride and took the bus in the rest of the way.'

And although he was still talking, just like in a film the sound of Jarvis's dad's voice faded and the sound of my thoughts took its place, '*He could drive. Jarvis could drive!*'

All those lifts.

The bastard.

'How long has he been driving?' I said.

'About four years now. Took him quite a few gos to pass. I don't think he was the easiest of pupils to teach to be honest. And the insurance was astronomical.' He took his rubber gloves off and stuck them on top of the cold tap. 'He *would* insist on putting actor as his profession on the application form.'

Jarvis's dad told me about how actors paid some of the highest insurance premiums and something about someone at an insurance company saying that one of the reasons the insurance was so high for actors was that there was always the possibility that because of his job Jarvis might end up giving a lift to Julia Roberts or Tom Cruise. Jarvis would have loved hearing that.

I left Jarvis to order the drinks in the last remaining Mister Breakfast and I walked back to my car and phoned PC Buss.

For a million pounds would you grass on your best friend?

I could have just driven away and left him there I suppose. Maybe he'd never kill again. It was the beginning of August. Perhaps he'd be ill or busy in a month's time and miss his kill-by-date.

And if he stuck to his MO he'd have to stop soon anyway. He only had one murder venue left and it was always too full with people, it was brightly lit with a fully functioning CCTV system and had a policeman in the foyer.

But this month it would be the fifteenth anniversary of Diana's death. Surely Jarvis would feel compelled to mark the date somehow – even if he had to change his regular crime location – kill somebody at a steak house or a noodle bar. I couldn't let myself be in any way responsible for a 2012 entry in Jarvis's September murder diary.

What if it had all been my fault that he'd killed in the first place? It all happened during my absence. Now I was back behind the wheel maybe he'd just stop. I could go back in to the restaurant now, drink my coffee and somehow just forget about it all.

That was impossible of course.

Maybe I should have Thelma and Louise'd the Nissan Micra off the M5 and down onto the Holiday and Retirement Village below. I didn't want to upset my girlfriend though by writing off our new car. I'd already lost her umbrella.

She wasn't going to be happy that I'd lied to her about Jarvis not being able to drive. Or that I'd knowingly got into the car with a murderer. Why hadn't I just called the police as soon as I found the diary in the cake tin? she'd say.

When I tell her I'd thought it would be a good idea to bring Jarvis to the last surviving Mister Breakfast to give the story a proper ending, she'd be furious.

I should have been scared I suppose: having a killer in the back of the car. But I wasn't. My girlfriend would never understand when I told her that it was only Jarvis.

Both my girlfriend and the police would want to know why I hadn't suspected Jarvis earlier, why I hadn't noticed something not quite right about him. And I'd really want to make a joke out of everything being not quite right about Jarvis, and how was I supposed to pick out one thing amongst all that other stuff? I never once suspected him though. Maybe I'm dense. Maybe Jarvis is a better actor than I thought he was.

I've tried to find a suitable analogy for finding out your friend is a murderer. I came up with a couple.

1. It's like discovering your all time favourite singer votes Conservative or eats veal.
2. It's like being on a long taxi journey with a hilarious taxi driver who keeps you entertained right up until two minutes from your destination when he denies the Holocaust.

There is, I decided, no suitable analogy for finding out your friend is a murderer.

I looked over at the Mister Breakfast. I could see Jarvis sitting at a table, pushing the plunger of his cafetiere too soon. He always did that. No patience. I heard sirens in the distance. The police would be kicking in the door of the holiday home round about now.

It was best for everyone this way. No more deaths, Jarvis gets the fame he's always craved and I get to write something longer than a church sign or a Christmas cracker joke. Maybe not quite as funny, but longer at least.

If I was Jarvis Ham's manager I was going to be the greatest manager ever. I'd give my client everything he'd always dreamed about. His life would be serialised in the newspapers and talked about on television for years to come. He'd have his own Wikipedia page. Journalists and photographers would be outside the court on step-ladders calling out his name. He'd get his epileptic fit warning on the News. Jarvis would probably even get to turn the prison Christmas lights on.

I might have to drop the opening lines about eating poo and the bit about Jarvis masturbating when his mother died, and I might add thirty pages or so at the start on what Jarvis's grandparents got up to during the First World War, but other than that I think he'd be happy.

It was going to be brilliant.

Very brilliant.

ACKNOWLEDGEMENTS

Thanks to Nicola Barr, Scott Pack, Corinna Harrod, Jacqueline, Holly, Neil Witherow, Marc Ollington, Les Carter, Tim Connery, Chris T-T, Jonathan and Justine Bookseller Crow, Andrew Collins, Michael Legge, John Facundo, Robin Ince, Sarah Bennetto, James Dowdeswell, Chris Addison, Dave Gorman, Scroobius Pip, Isy Suttie, Eddie Argos, Jo Neary, Todd and Suzanne at Literary Death Match, Martin White, Danielle Ward, Johny Lamb, Ben Murray, Steve Lamacq, Miles and Erica, everyone at TFP, my mum, and to Becca, Addison, Jake, Madeline, Ryan and all the other lovely people of the South Hams.

This copy of Driving Jarvis Ham comes with a free download of the Day Job E.P. featuring four brand new songs by Jim Bob. To stream or download the E.P. please visit:

www.harpercollins.co.uk/drivingjarvisham

And follow the simple instructions.

Enjoy!